The broad-shouldered cowboy blocked her exit. "You're not going anywhere. You have to start thinking about yourself and your baby."

Mona told herself she couldn't breathe because of how tightly Reed held her, but the truth was that her breathing was short and shallow because her body burned. "You're just the hired help. Why do you care?"

"I just do." Then he was kissing her, hard and long. Before she could begin to think, his hands were combing through her hair, bringing her lips impossibly closer.

When his lips tore free, she stared up at him, her eyes wide, her breathing ragged. What had he just done to her? He'd made her completely forget for a moment anything to do with Rancho Linda and her heritage. For a moment all she wanted was for him to kiss her again.

Then the baby kicked against her belly hard enough to make her jerk.

ELLE JAMES

TEXAS-SIZED SECRETS

HARLEQUIN®

TORONTO • NEW YORK • LONDON
AMSTERDAM • PARIS • SYDNEY • HAMBURG
STOCKHOLM • ATHENS • TOKYO • MILAN • MADRID
PRAGUE • WARSAW • BUDAPEST • AUCKLAND

To Megan Kerans, thanks for sending me the article about cattle rustling. Thanks to all my family and friends who help feed my writing habit with great new ideas.

ISBN-13: 978-0-373-88826-9
ISBN-10:   0-373-88826-0

TEXAS-SIZED SECRETS

Copyright © 2008 by Mary Jernigan

www.eHarlequin.com

Printed in U.S.A.

ABOUT THE AUTHOR

A 2004 Golden Heart Award winner for Best Paranormal Romance, Elle James started writing when her sister issued the Y2K challenge to write a romance novel. She managed a full-time job, raised three wonderful children and she and her husband even tried their hands at ranching exotic birds (ostriches, emus, and rheas) in the Texas hill country. Ask her, and she'll tell you, what it's like to go toe-to-toe with an angry 350-pound bird! After leaving her successful career in information technology management, Elle is now pursuing her writing full-time. She loves building exciting stories about heroes, heroines, romance and passion. Elle loves to hear from fans. You can contact her at ellejames@earthlink.net or visit her Web site at www.ellejames.com.

Books by Elle James

HARLEQUIN INTRIGUE
906—BENEATH THE TEXAS MOON
938—DAKOTA MELTDOWN
961—LAKOTA BABY
987—COWBOY SANCTUARY
1014—BLOWN AWAY
1033—ALASKAN FANTASY
1052—TEXAS-SIZED SECRETS

Don't miss any of our special offers. Write to us at the following address for information on our newest releases.

Harlequin Reader Service
U.S.: 3010 Walden Ave., P.O. Box 1325, Buffalo, NY 14269
Canadian: P.O. Box 609, Fort Erie, Ont. L2A 5X3

CAST OF CHARACTERS

Reed Bryson—Ex-Chicago cop, ex-deputy for the Briscoe County Sheriff's department, Reed follows his instincts and does what it takes to protect the people who need protection.

Mona Grainger—This proud and pregnant ranch owner will do anything to protect her family, her heritage and her ranch. She'd even advertise for a gun-for-hire to rid her land of cattle rustlers, who threaten to steal her livelihood.

Sheriff Parker Lee—The sheriff had his heart set on owning Mona and her ranch. What deep dark secrets does he hide behind his badge?

Arty Grainger—Mona's uncle never forgave her father for marrying a Mexican woman. Is his anger for his dead brother enough to make him seek revenge on Mona?

Dusty Gaither—Mona's hot-headed ranch hand. Who does he really work for?

Jeffrey Kuhn—Prairie Rock banker with some Texas-sized secrets and a legal way to take Mona's land.

Patricia Teague—Wealthy widow and owner of an oil speculation company. Why'd she choose Prairie Rock as her target for oil exploration? What does she have to gain?

Catalina Garcia—Mona's friend and surrogate sister who would deny her heritage to make her way in a tough world.

Chapter One

Wanted: Cowboy. Must be able to ride, rope and fence. Can't be afraid of hard work and long hours. Most of all, must know how to handle a gun. Position considered dangerous. See M. Grainger at the Rancho Linda.

The want ad sounded more like something out of the Wild West, not the new millennium. Who the hell advertised for a hired gun in this day and age? And how many nutcases would come out of the hills in response?

Reed Bryson stared one last time at the crumpled paper before he stepped down from his truck. Jobs were scarce in Briscoe County. It wasn't as if he had a lot of choices.

For the second time this year he was interviewing for work. Although he'd gone thirteen years without riding a horse, he knew he'd have no trouble riding. Roping would come back, and moving cattle was as natural as breathing to him despite the time lapse. He met all the requirements of the job notice he'd picked up at Dee's Diner. Even the last one. Twelve years on the Chicago police force had honed his ability to fire a gun and to know when.

A shiny white dually stood next to his truck with Teague Oil & Gas printed on the doors. He'd seen the truck in Prairie Rock over the past couple months. Oil speculators were as thick as horseflies in the panhandle.

He settled his Stetson on his head and strode to the two-story, white, wood frame house. It probably dated back to the nineteenth century, with its wide wrap-around porches, tall windows and doors designed to catch the breeze. A place built for air movement back when air conditioners weren't yet invented.

The front door was open, with the screen door firmly in place to keep the pesky horseflies out.

When Reed raised his hand and knocked, two men in tailored business suits appeared in the doorway.

"We'll be back tomorrow same time. Hopefully, Grainger can meet with us then." They stepped through the screen, each running a narrow-eyed glance over Reed as they descended from the porch without so much as a howdy-do. They climbed into the pickup and drove off, leaving a trail of dust floating over the prairie grass.

Footsteps echoed in the foyer and a short, plump Hispanic woman smiled a greeting. *"Buenos días, señor."*

"Habla inglés?"

"Sí. I speak very good English. What can I do for you?" Her English was excellent and laced with a charming hint of Mexican accent. She opened the door and held it with her hip while she dried wet hands on her apron.

"I'm here to see Mr. Grainger about the job."

The woman's gaze followed the dually as it left. When the oilmen disappeared out of sight, she switched her perusal to him, her glance traveling from hat to boots before she spoke again. "Check with my husband down by the barn. He'll know where to find the boss."

"Thank you, ma'am."

"De nada."

As Reed rounded the corner of the house, he could feel the woman's gaze following him. He couldn't blame her. After the oil speculators' visit, he'd be cautious too, as he was with all salesmen.

The barn stood two hundred yards from the house. As Reed approached, a dark-haired, dark-skinned man led a bay mare out of the building. The man stopped as he cleared the doorway and turned to adjust the saddle girth beneath the horse's belly.

"Excuse me." Reed slowed as he approached.

The man looked up and nodded, but continued tightening the strap.

"I'm looking for Mr. Grainger. I'm here about the job."

The man's brows rose up his forehead. "I'm going there now. Saddle up, you can come along." He led Reed into the dark interior of the barn and stopped in front of the second stall. A black horse with a white star on his forehead leaned over the stall door. "You ride Diablo."

When Reed hesitated, the man smiled.

"Don't worry. His name is worse than his reputation." A chuckle echoed through the interior of the big barn.

"That's good to know."

The man held out a hand. "I'm Fernando Garcia, the foreman." His words rolled off his tongue with the natural ease of one who'd grown up speaking Spanish as his first language.

"Reed Bryson." He clasped the man's hand in a firm handshake. Then he moved to the stall, holding out his fingers for the horse to sniff.

"Careful, amigo, he may not be a devil to ride, but he's been known to have a helluva bite."

Reed jerked his hand back and opened the stall door. He snagged the horse's halter and led him out into the center aisle.

Fernando tossed a blanket over the gelding's back and followed with a saddle. Reed quickly cinched the saddle in place and slid a bridle over the horse's head, slipping the bit between stubbornly clamped teeth.

Fernando nodded. "I'll wait outside. We need to

hurry, it's getting close to dark and I haven't seen the boss in a couple hours."

Reed braced a boot in a stirrup and swung his right leg over the saddle. When he emerged into the waning sunlight, he blinked at the brightness after being in the dark interior of the barn.

As soon as Reed exited the barn, Fernando took off.

Reed pressed his heels into Diablo's flanks and the beast took off at a gallop. As if it hadn't been thirteen years since Reed had been on the back of a horse, he settled into the smooth rhythm. He urged his mount forward until he rode side by side with Fernando.

Galloping wasn't the best time to quiz the man, but Reed wanted to know more about the job before he committed to it—*if* the boss saw fit to hire him. "Has there been trouble on the ranch?"

"*Sí.*" The foreman either was in a big hurry or he wasn't sharing what kind of trouble. The older man nudged his horse faster, racing across the low range grasses of the Texas panhandle.

Knowing he wasn't getting any more information out of the man, Reed dropped back, content to follow. His questions would be answered soon enough by the ranch owner himself.

Fernando topped a rise and dropped down behind it.

When Reed reached the top of the slope, his heart leaped into his throat at the steep drop on the other side.

As if anxious to catch the other horse, Diablo danced to the side, straining against the reins.

"Okay, go for it." Reed gave the horse his head and held on while the animal plunged downward into a small canyon tangled with a maze of ravines and fallen rocks.

He thought he heard someone's shouts echoing off the canyon walls, but the sound of the horse's hooves slipping and sliding down the rocky path could have been playing tricks on his hearing.

Fernando had eased his horse into a walk, picking his way through the rocks and bramble that spooked his mount. With the skill of one born to ride, the man held his seat and urged his mount to continue down the hill to the bottom of the canyon.

A riderless horse passed Reed and leaped over the top of the hill behind him. He assumed it was the boss's horse and spurred his own forward at a lethal pace for the downhill slide.

When Reed reached the canyon floor, he just caught a glimpse of Fernando's horse rounding the corner of a sheer bluff wall.

Without hesitation, Reed dug his heels into the horse's flanks and raced after him, wondering, not for the first time, if this was some kind of test or trap. He reached beneath his denim jacket and flicked the safety strap off his Glock. Whether he was being led into an ambush or the boss of the Rancho Linda was really in trouble, he'd be ready.

When he rounded yet another corner of rocky wall, he pulled up sharply, narrowly avoiding a collision with Fernando and his mount.

Diablo reared and screamed.

Fernando's bay mare danced to the side but refused to go forward.

Ahead a hundred yards was a cow, lying on her side, clearly in the midst of a birthing gone bad. In front of her was a herd of wild hogs. Between the downed cow and the canyon wall stood a small woman with flowing black hair and brown-black eyes. She waved her straw cowboy hat at the angry animals and yelled. As small as she was, she wasn't making much of an impression on the three-hundred-pound swine circling her and the distressed cow.

Fernando pulled his rifle from the scabbard on the front of his saddle and aimed it in the air. A round exploded, the sound echoing off the canyon walls.

While most of the hogs jumped and scattered, a few of the larger, more aggressive males turned their attention from the girl to Fernando. Fearless, or too mad to care, two of the beasts charged.

The older man's horse reared and spun. In order to stay in the saddle, Fernando had to drop the rifle and hold on. His horse lit out with several of the hogs in pursuit.

Reed's horse danced to the side behind a stand of rocks. A scream ripped across the canyon walls, chilling his blood.

The largest of the boars rammed into the cow's swollen belly. The cow bellowed and tried to roll to her feet. With a calf lodged in the birthing canal, she wasn't going anywhere.

The woman behind the cow shouted and waved her hat. "Get the hell away from her. Get!"

What did she hope to accomplish? Her little bit of flapping served as a red cape waved in front of a bull. The boar lowered his tusks and rammed the cow again.

The woman leaned across the cow's belly and beat at the boar's snout.

"Move back!" Reed shouted. "Move back!" He leaped to the ground, yanking his pistol from the holster beneath his arm.

"No! Don't hurt the cow!"

The boar rammed the cow again.

Since the woman still leaned over the downed bovine, the force of the boar's impact catapulted her backward. She hit the rock wall behind her, sliding down to land hard on her butt.

When the boar backed away, preparing for another charge, Reed aimed at the hog's head and fired.

The hog dropped where it stood.

Reed raced to where the woman sat, rubbing the back of her head, her eyes glazed.

"You all right?" He held out a hand.

She ignored him and scrambled to her feet. "Move!" Shoving him to the side, she ran a few steps along the base of the bluff before doubling over and throwing up in the dirt.

Reed hurried over to her and held her hair out of her face until she was done, hesitantly patting her back. He wasn't sure what to do. Something inside him made him want to comfort this woman who'd gone through a particularly scary event.

When she straightened, her face was pale, but her lips were firm. She looked like a woman with a tentative grasp on her control and the determination to maintain it. "Can you give me a hand with the calf? It's stillborn and stuck."

Reed stared into her eyes until he was sure she was going to remain on her feet, then he turned to the laboring cow.

He'd seen this happen before when a cow tried to give birth to a calf too big for the birth canal. Half the time, they lost cow and calf. With the calf already dead, the best they could hope for was to save the cow.

He sat in the dirt behind the cow, braced his feet against the animal's backside and grabbed hold of the dead calf's legs.

Too tired and battered to help, the cow lay on her side, breathing hard. When the next contraction hit, she bellowed, and tried to push with what little strength she had left.

Reed pulled with all his might. The calf slid out a little farther.

"You're doing good." The woman squatted

beside the cow and smoothed a hand over her head. "Hang in there."

Another contraction rolled over the cow's belly and her legs stretched straight out, her stomach muscles convulsing.

Reaching down to the calf's shoulders, Reed tugged as hard as he could and the calf slid out the rest of the way.

For several long moments, the cow and Reed gathered their strength. Then the cow rolled to a sitting position and nudged the dead calf.

"Sorry, girl, this baby didn't make it." The woman patted the cow's neck.

While the cow licked at the calf's face, Reed stood and wiped his hands on his jeans.

The woman straightened, the top of her head only coming up to Reed's shoulders. "You here about the job?"

"Yes, ma'am."

She walked around the cow to stand beside the dead boar. "Was I mistaken or did you drop that boar with one shot?"

"You were not mistaken, ma'am."

She dusted her hands on her jeans and reached out. "I'm Mona Grainger. You're hired."

Chapter Two

The man with the sandy-blond hair, moss-green eyes and a square jawline stood with his cowboy hat in hand, staring at her. "You're M. Grainger? The owner of the Rancho Linda?"

She had to give this guy a little credit. He asked without the usual shocked look. "That would be me." She'd gotten the shocked response from all the applicants thus far. They expected a wiry, grizzled hulk of a man like her father. Not a petite young woman who barely topped five feet three inches.

Her father had died less than a year ago in a riding accident, leaving her as the sole surviving heir to the ranch. She couldn't change her sex or size. What you saw was what you got. "Do you have a problem answering to a female boss?"

"Not at all." He grinned. "I just didn't expect M. Grainger to be so…pretty." He stuck out his hand. "Reed Bryson." He glanced at his dirty hand. "Never mind."

When he started to drop his hand, she grabbed it and shook it with as firm a grip as she could muster. She may be small, but she didn't want him to think she wasn't tough. "A little dirt never hurt me."

Now that she had time to really study him, she wasn't as pleased as she'd been at first to hire him. Although not exactly what she'd hoped for, Mr. Bryson had proven he could ride and shoot, and he hadn't balked at helping a cow with a stillborn calf. The roping part could be taught. It was the rest of the package that bothered her.

Mona's gaze ran the long length of the cowboy who stood at least six feet two in his faded denim jeans and blue chambray shirt. A twinge of apprehension gnawed at her now-empty gut. She didn't like men who were too good to look at. She'd fallen into that trap before and she sure as hell wasn't going there again. Some mistakes were harder to live with than others.

Reed dropped her hand and squatted next to the boar. "Should be good eating. Want me to fieldstrip him?"

The stench of the hog wrapped around her olfactory nerves and her stomach rebelled. For the second time in the past ten minutes, she ran a couple steps and then hurled the last of the contents of her belly.

"On second thought, why don't we get you back to the house. I can come back here later and take care of him and check on the cow."

Fernando raced around the corner, brought his

horse to a skidding halt and dropped to the ground. "Miss Mona, are you all right?" He hurried across the floor of the canyon and wrapped an arm around the woman as if she would break.

With a grimace, she pushed him away. "I'm all right. Nothing's broken."

He snatched her hat from the ground and pounded it against his leg before he handed it to her. A deep frown marred his dark forehead. "You should have waited for me to come help you with the cow. It's not something a—"

"I'm fine." She shot a glance at Reed. Fernando worried too much about her and her condition. Let the new hand get adjusted to working for a woman before he learned more about her.

Her foreman followed her glance and nodded. "This kind of work takes more than one to accomplish. Especially when you're in the canyons. Wild boars aren't the only animals you have to worry about."

She knew all too well the risks. But she refused to lose any more livestock to man or beast. Mona turned to the new hand. "When can you start?"

"It seems I've already started." He glanced down at his dirty jeans and the cow, just lumbering to her feet. "Is today all right with you?"

"Perfect. How are you for working nights?"

"I spent twelve years on the force in Chicago and the past few months as a deputy for Briscoe County. I know how to pull night duty, but tell me—" Reed frowned "—what kind of cattle ranching are you doing at night?"

Her rosy lips twisted. "Call it ranch security." She turned to Fernando. "I don't suppose Sassy stopped at the edge of the canyon, did she?"

"No. She's probably back at the barn by now." He removed his toe from the left stirrup. "You take the saddle. I'll ride behind."

With her bottom bruised from the fall, Mona didn't argue. She stretched high to reach the saddle horn. Before she knew it, hands grasped her waist and lifted her into the saddle. Hands bigger and stronger than Fernando's.

Heat filled her cheeks as she fitted her boots into the stirrups. She hadn't had someone lift her so effortlessly into a saddle since she was a little girl. And damned if she didn't like it a little too much. A frown settled between her brows. "I can manage on my own."

"Yes, ma'am. I reckon you can, but my mamma taught me to help a lady. It's kind of a habit." As he stared up at her, a smile tipped the corners of his lips.

Her insides warmed, the heat spreading up her neck. Then a gray haze filtered her vision, blackness creeping around the edges. Oh no. Not again.

The blackness claimed her.

"ARE YOU SURE you're up to this tonight?" Reed sat behind the wheel of the ranch pickup truck, bumping along the dirt road that ran parallel to the inside of the fence.

"Look, I didn't hire you to give me advice. I needed a ranch hand, period." He was learning fast, Mona Grainger didn't mince words.

"Normally I wouldn't worry about another human being except you happened to get knocked on your butt by an angry hog today and then you passed out. And you haven't even had a doctor check you out for concussion." He'd carried her all the way back to the ranch house on his horse before she'd woken up. Despite their brief acquaintance, he'd been scared half to death for her. With her limp body leaning against his the entire way, he'd had too much time to think up reasons for her to pass out and none of them were good.

"I was hungry and tired. That's all. Besides, we're not riding horses. What we need to do tonight can be accomplished in a truck. I didn't ask to drive, so drop the worried-employee act. If I pass out, you won't be required to carry me anywhere."

"I didn't mind carrying you." Hell, his hands still tingled from lifting her into the saddle and holding her snuggly against his chest. Her hips were narrow, she had a cute bit of a belly, but she didn't weigh much more than a bale of hay. How could someone so small be so tough…and so sexy? Her long black hair had hung to her waist in wavy disarray. He could tell by the crease at her nape that she must have had it secured earlier in a ponytail. Though he liked it loose.

The long strands had brushed against his face when he'd lifted her into the saddle. Silky smooth and smelling of prairie grass. A man could lose himself in her scent. Reed shifted in his seat, disturbed by the direction of his thoughts.

Focusing on his surroundings, he committed to memory the few landmarks he could see in the fading light. Once away from the ranch house and its lone stand of trees planted as a windbreak, the terrain looked pretty much the same. Gently rolling plains stretched for miles with not another tree in sight. With the window down to let in the cool night air, the smell of dry grass and sagebrush filled the interior of the truck. The scent brought back recollections of growing up on his father's ranch just a county over from Briscoe.

He had to admit they weren't all bad memories. He'd had free run of thousands of acres, and a horse he could escape on whenever he got the chance. For that reason he missed his father's ranch. Too bad his father didn't own it anymore.

Mona's hand reached out and touched his sleeve. "Slow down." She pointed to a slight rise in the prairie. "Park the truck behind that hill and turn off the lights."

He pressed the brake, slowing the truck to a halt at the same time as he flicked the lights off. For several moments, they sat in the dark, until their eyes adjusted.

When Mona opened the door, Reed's hand shot

out. "I know you told me ranch security, but what exactly do you mean by that?"

She stared at his hand until he released her arm. "We've had several instances of cattle rustling in the past month. With over six thousand acres of land to manage, I can't do it all on my own. There are too many places to be at once." She grabbed her rifle from the gun rack behind her head and slid off the truck seat, dropping to the ground.

Reed reached for his rifle and followed suit. "Why don't you go to the sheriff?" Not that he'd trust the sheriff to handle anything more than a speeding ticket.

"No." No explanation, no reasons.

Mona Grainger moved up a notch in Reed's esteem. He didn't care for Sheriff Parker Lee. "Okay, if not the sheriff, why not the DPS?"

An unladylike snort escaped her. "Public Safety referred me to local law enforcement." As she neared the top of the small rise, she knelt in the grass and dropped to her hands and knees, inching toward the ridgeline.

Following her lead, Reed did the same until he'd crawled up beside her in the grass. A moonless night had settled in, with a million stars lighting the heavens. On the other side of the hill, a dark ribbon of road stretched for miles, disappearing in the blackness.

As his eyes adjusted to the darkness, Reed made out tiny red dots in the distance just as they disappeared over the horizon. Possibly the blink of brake lights on a tractor-trailer rig.

"Did you see that?" Mona asked.

"Yeah."

"Hundred bucks says that's a truck full of Rancho Linda cattle." She stood and fired a shot at the retreating vehicle, not that her rifle had that kind of distance.

An answering shot echoed through the darkness.

Reed grabbed Mona and pulled her to the ground.

"Some of them are still down there. I'd like to keep my job for longer than a day, if you don't mind."

The sound of a small engine revving carried across the hill.

"Come on!" Mona leaped to her feet and scrambled back down the slope to the truck.

Right behind her, Reed climbed into the truck and switched it to four-wheel drive. They topped the hill doing thirty and plunged downward to the field below.

Taillights glowed red on the road over a mile away. The rustlers had a head start on them. If they had any kind of horsepower in their vehicle, they'd be gone before Reed and Mona made the highway.

"Damn." Mona held on to the handle above the door as the truck bounced over uneven terrain, small bushes and rocks on its descent to the bottom of the hill.

Meanwhile, the taillights disappeared into the night.

Reed eased across the cut barbed-wire fence, careful not to get wire wrapped around the axles.

When he pulled up onto the pavement, he turned to Mona. "Want me to follow?"

"Hell, yeah." Mona slammed her palm against the armrest. "They can't get away with this. Those are my cattle."

With the lead the rustlers had, Reed didn't think they had a chance, but he gunned the truck and flew down the road, gaining speed until the pickup traveled at over one hundred miles per hour. For the next thirty minutes, they raced over deserted highways and back roads, but the truck and tractor-trailer rig had disappeared.

When he came to a crossroad where the county road T-junctioned onto a state highway, Reed pulled to a stop and turned to his new boss. "Which way?"

Instead of looking at the highway stretching to the left or right, she stared straight ahead across an open field in front of them. The lights from the dash glinted off the moisture in her eyes. Once again, her hair had escaped the confines of the elastic band she'd worn earlier and laid across her shoulders in shiny waves of ebony.

Tempted to reach out and touch the strands, Reed gripped the steering wheel tighter. He wanted to comfort her, give her reason to hang on. Something told him she wouldn't appreciate any sympathy from him or any other man.

She sat there, her jaw firmed, her lips thinning into a straight line. "In case you haven't gotten the hint, this is the reason why I hired you. Tomorrow we come up with a plan to stop these thieves. Do you still want the job?"

More than ever. The challenge excited him, almost as much as his new boss. "Yes."

"Good. Now, if you'll excuse me." She opened the door, climbed down from the truck and threw up in the ditch.

Chapter Three

"Just like you said, the fences were cut and there were tire tracks in the dirt by the road. Other than that, we didn't find any other evidence." Sheriff Parker Lee stood with his hat still firmly planted on his head, despite being indoors. A smug look barely hid beneath the surface of his painted-on concern.

Mona's stomach burbled, the acid churning nonstop since Parker Lee stepped through her door. She swore she'd never let him set foot on her property in her lifetime. But then tough times called for compromises. "You can't tell me you're still clueless. That's three hits in the past month." Mona stopped midway across the living room to face the one man she hated more than any other. "What's it gonna take to get you to do something about this problem?"

The sheriff stepped forward and laid his hands on her shoulders. "Now, Mona, if you'd just let me take care of you like I promised, none of this would be happening."

Her anger turned to deep dark rage. If her eyes could shoot venom, she'd have poisoned Parker Lee with one look. "Get your hands off me."

"Mona..." His fingers tightened on her arms until they hurt.

Mona cocked her knee, ready to plant it square in his groin.

"The lady told you to get your hands off her." Reed pushed through the screen door and entered the room. He stood with his feet braced apart, his cowboy hat in one hand.

"Bryson." Sheriff Lee's eyes narrowed. "I didn't expect you to be out here. I thought you headed back to Chicago."

"Hardly."

Mona shot a look at Reed. She'd hired him on the spot without so much as an interview. She knew nothing else about this man. "He's with me."

"You do know Bryson here was a deputy for all of five months before I fired him. Can't have a deputy who refuses to follow orders." Lee's brows rose. "Ain't that right?"

Reed's lips thinned, but he refused to answer, although his gaze remained on Sheriff Lee.

Mona liked him all the more for not rising to Parker Lee's bait. She couldn't claim the same amount of restraint. Too often she'd come close to scratching the man's eyes out. A purely female reaction to a lying, deceiving man. Thank God she was over him.

"Mona? What's goin' on here?" A booming voice sounded outside on the porch before her uncle Arty pushed through the doorway. "What's the sheriff doin' here?"

Her two ranch hands, Dusty Gaither and Jesse Lopez, followed him in.

"Pardon, Miss Mona," Jesse said. "He insisted on coming in."

Oh great. Now they could have one happy hoedown. The dry cereal she'd forced herself to eat that morning threatened to come up. "Someone made off with thirty head of Rancho Linda cattle."

"Told your daddy to leave this place to me. Ain't right to saddle a girl with this much responsibility."

Mona's head hurt and she didn't want to take anything for the pain, but the pain was making her stomach act up.

Rosa Garcia, her housekeeper and surrogate mother, appeared by her side with a tray of lemonade and crackers. "Eat this," she whispered.

The thought of putting anything past her lips made her even more nauseous, but if she didn't, she'd be sick in front of all three men. Mona lifted a cracker and a glass of lemonade. "Thank you."

"I've tried to tell her the same. She needs a man around here." The sheriff's chest puffed out as if to say he was the one who should fill that role.

Mona swallowed her cracker in two bites, choking

on what Parker Lee implied. "I can manage the ranch on my own."

Uncle Arty snorted. "Do you call losing thirty cattle managing? How many did you lose last week? Twenty more? You can't manage a six-thousand-acre ranch with just a few Mexicans. For all you know, they're the ones stealing from you."

Mona set her glass on the table with a thump. "Watch it, Uncle. You're forgetting I'm half Mexican." She marched across the room and stood toe-to-toe with the man. "You may not have liked it that my father married a Mexican, but he loved my mother and she loved him. You should be so lucky to have that kind of relationship."

Her uncle didn't back down a bit. "What do you know? She died when you were little. I still think my brother only married her to spite our father."

"Get out." Mona stood with one hand fisted on her hip, the other pointing to the doorway.

"Now, you listen to me, girl," her uncle blustered. "I don't like that tone of voice."

"Get. Out." If she had to use a gun, she would. Uncle or no, he had no right to bad-mouth her father, God rest his soul.

"So be it." Her uncle stalked across the room and turned when he reached the door. He jabbed a finger at her. "You're going to run this place into the ground. You mark my words."

"Maybe so, but it's my place to run into the ground, not yours."

"This land has been in the Grainger family for over one hundred years and should have stayed in the family. You're nothin' but a girl. You don't stand a chance. When it goes up in smoke, don't expect me to bail you out."

REED OPENED the screen for Mona's uncle, his brows high on his forehead. "You were leaving?"

"Don't get smart with me, young man. You'll be out of work within a week and I can guarantee you won't find another job in this county."

With a smile plastered to his face, Reed waved toward the open door, refusing to rise to the man's threat.

Once Mona's uncle left, Reed turned to the sheriff, his anger rising. A useless excuse for law enforcement, Parker Lee wouldn't survive a day on the Chicago police force. He'd be shot in the back by one of his own men. Then again, he'd never have been hired. Lee didn't have what it took—integrity.

"You shouldn't be so hard on your uncle. He's right, you know." Sheriff Lee turned a sneering glance at Reed. "I'm surprised Mona hired you. Especially since you can't seem to hold a job."

To Reed's surprise, Mona's face softened into a sensual smile. "Who said I hired him?" She walked across the floor and hooked an arm around Reed's waist. "Reed lives here."

With supreme effort, Reed forced his expression to be casual, calm, not flat-out shocked. He pulled her close against him and dropped a kiss to the top of her hair. No perfumes clogged his senses, just the simple smell of soap and herbal shampoo rose up to greet him. She fit against him like she was meant to be there. He kinda liked it. "Do we need to spell it out for you?" He stared across the wooden floor at Parker Lee.

A muscle in the sheriff's jaw twitched before he responded. "Just remember, she was mine before she even knew you."

Mona's body tensed against Reed's. "I was never *yours*. Any relationship we might have had is in the past. And, trust me, I'll always remember it as a huge lapse in my judgment."

The man's face burned a mottled red before he turned on his heel and marched through the door. Without another word, he climbed into the custom SUV with Sheriff painted in bold letters on each side and spun out of the gravel driveway.

"I don't suppose he'll be of much help finding the cattle rustlers, do you?" Mona stared after the sheriff, still standing in the curve of Reed's arm. Then as if she remembered where she was, she stepped away, her face coloring a pretty shade of rosy pink beneath her natural tan. "I'm sorry. I just put you on the spot." A smile curved her lips, humor adding a twinkle to her deep brown-black eyes. "Thanks for going along with my little ruse."

"So, you and Sheriff Lee were an item?"

"Over five months ago. And we only went out for a month. I wouldn't call us an item."

"Still, he thinks he has squatting rights."

"Some men don't get the hint, even when it's flung square in their faces. Parker Lee considers me one of his conquests and he doesn't like to lose." She shrugged. "I'm afraid I've made you a powerful enemy in this county."

"I'm not sweating it. I've seen how the sheriff operates."

"Yeah, that's right. I don't remember seeing you on the police force."

"I worked nights."

"Why'd you quit?"

"I had my reasons."

She nodded. "I get it. Don't ask."

"Do you have any regrets knowing I quit the sheriff's department?"

"No. In fact it makes me even more certain I hired the right man. Since I opened my mouth to Parker, you'd better move your gear from the bunkhouse into the main house. Rosa!"

The small Hispanic woman stood framed in the doorway as if she'd anticipated Mona's call. *"Sí, hija."*

"Mr. Bryson will be staying in the house. Would you mind putting fresh sheets on the guest bed?"

The older woman shot Reed a penetrating look. "Are you sure he can be trusted?"

Mona tipped her head to the side and stared at Reed. "Can you?"

With her looking at him with a spark in her dark eyes, Reed wasn't so sure himself. She was beautiful in both an earthy and exotic way, with no need for makeup or fancy clothing. At that moment, he wanted to leave before he did something stupid like develop a hankerin' for this woman who insisted on waging a battle against all odds. But to leave her now didn't sit right in Reed's book. She was one woman trying to do it all.

"I'm a man of my word." He shifted his hat to his other hand. "Now let me get this straight. My job is to help find your cattle rustlers?"

"That's right."

"What about Parker Lee?"

"If you don't mind, I'd appreciate it if you'd continue playing the part of my live-in to keep him off my back."

Not that he wanted anything out of her but his paycheck, but Reed couldn't help asking, "What's in it for me?"

"You get to eat Rosa's good cooking instead of fending for yourself with the boys in the bunkhouse."

Reed's mouth twisted. "Having had the opportunity to taste their cooking, I'd be honored to pretend to be your boyfriend."

Rosa crossed her arms over her chest. "Just remember, there are three people in this house besides you. Don't try anything with Miss Mona, or you'll have to answer to me."

"Yes, ma'am." He turned to Mona. "Is there anything else I should know?"

Mona chewed her lip for a moment before shaking her head. "No."

"Yes, there is." Rosa moved forward to stand beside Mona. "Tell him."

"No." Mona's face flushed and a thin sheen of perspiration coated her skin. "It's none of his business."

Curious now, Reed waited.

"If he's to help protect you and Rancho Linda, he needs to know everything."

"That's right." Reed didn't like the way Mona fidgeted. What else was she hiding?

"No." She wrapped an arm around her belly, her face turning a sickly shade of gray-green. "None of the hands know and the fewer people who do know the better."

Rosa grabbed Mona's arms. "You can't continue to ignore the fact and, if you're not careful, you'll hurt yourself and…others. Look at you. You can't even keep food down."

"It doesn't change anything. I still have a job to do and I *will* find the cattle rustlers."

"You need to tell him."

"No." Tears welled in her eyes and she shot a

panicked look at Reed. "Ah hell." Mona clamped a hand to her mouth and ran from the room.

Reed could hear her being sick in the bathroom and he started to follow her.

A hand on his arm stopped him.

"Let me go. She's obviously sick." When he tried to move past the woman, her grip tightened. "What's wrong with her? That's the third time since we met she's lost it."

"Mr. Bryson. If you really want to help Miss Grainger, you need to understand…she's pregnant."

Chapter Four

"Good afternoon, Miss Grainger." Jeffrey Kuhn stood in the doorway of his office and waved her over. His graying blond hair and green eyes were set off by the light gray tailored suit he wore.

Something about his tanned skin and broad shoulders didn't fit the suit and tie. Having known the man for most of her life, Mona didn't understand why, all of the sudden, she'd think Kuhn didn't belong in the bank. "Hello, Mr. Kuhn."

"If you'd step into my office, we have matters to discuss."

"We do?" Mona had come to Prairie Rock to make the monthly mortgage payment on her land, not chat with the bank president. She had a lot of work to do back home. An uneasy twinge gripped her belly as if the baby tried to warn her something was amiss.

"Yes, we do." He waited until she entered his office and then closed the door behind her.

If she'd known she was going to have a business

meeting with the bank president she'd have worn something other than her usual jeans and denim shirt. Hell, she'd have left her hair loose instead of pulling it back into a juvenile ponytail. Mona resisted the urge to pat the dust off her clothing before she took the seat opposite the banker, a massive mahogany desk between them. "What is it you wanted to discuss?"

He stared at her for several seconds before beginning, as if sizing her up. "I understand you've had troubles out at the Rancho Linda?"

Mona fought to keep her expression blank. Cattle rustling in the area couldn't be kept a secret. Not when everyone knew everyone's business and the sheriff's blotter in the local newspaper was the highlight of the week. "Nothing we can't handle." She hoped. The rustlers had to slip up soon and be caught. Preferably before she went out of business.

"I couldn't help but notice your advertisement in the local gazette for a ranch hand." He planted his elbows on his desk and laced his fingers. "Or should I say, gun for hire?"

Mona sat up straighter. "Why do you ask?"

"As you well know, the bank has an interest in everything that goes on with their investments. If something were to happen to you or the ranch, we stand to lose money."

"That's true. But nothing is going to happen to me or the ranch."

"We at the bank disagree." He leaned forward.

"Advertising a gun-for-hire only reinforced our opinion that you're in over your head."

Did the man think her stupid? Was he carrying a mouse in his pocket? "We, or you, Mr. Kuhn?" Mona stood, anger pushing her blood pressure skyward. Not good for the baby.

His brows rose and he eased to his feet. "The bank, of course. Not me personally."

"Right." Mona held out the check she'd come to deliver. "I came to make my mortgage payment."

The man stuffed his hands in his pockets. "I'm afraid that isn't enough. You do realize your mortgage is on a seven-year adjustable-rate plan with a balloon note at the end, do you not?"

Mona stared at the banker for a full thirty seconds. She'd spent all of her time on the ranch in the saddle, not behind the desk. Her father handled the finances up until the day he died. When she took over, she'd only done what she had to do to make payments and keep money in the checking account. "No, I didn't realize. What does it mean?"

Kuhn's brows rose. "This is the end of the seven-year period. The balloon payment is due in less than thirty days."

"It is?" She swallowed, her throat dry as a desert. "Can't we roll it over into a fixed-rate loan?"

"I'm afraid not." He crossed his arms over his chest, his face blank of all emotion. "The bank doesn't consider you a good risk. You have thirty days to pay the balance in full or we begin foreclosure proceedings on the property."

The ground threatened to open up and suck in Mona. With more than a little effort, she fought off that dizzy, fuzzy-headed feeling and the encroaching blackness. Instead of fainting, she squared her shoulders and faced Mr. Kuhn. "You can't do that. We've done business with this bank ever since I can remember." How much was left on the loan? Thirty, forty, fifty thousand? No way could she come up with that kind of money.

"I'm sorry, Miss Grainger, but the decision has been made." He sat forward, resting his elbows on the desk. "Have you considered selling the ranch to someone more…capable?"

Mona's hackles rose. Even though she'd doubted her ability lately, she sure as hell wouldn't let Mr. Kuhn know that. "I'm perfectly *capable* of managing the ranch on my own."

"How about selling to one of the oil speculators here in town? I hear Lang Oil Exploration is acquiring property."

Stealing, more likely. Everyone who'd sold to Lang Oil lately had gotten the shaft in some way or other. And not an oil-drilling shaft.

Plucking up enough anger to make her voice strong, Mona stood. "Rancho Linda is not for sale. And for your information, I'm every bit as capable as my father was to run it."

"I'm afraid the bank doesn't see it that way. I'm sorry, but we won't be renewing your loan and we won't accept less than the payoff amount of fifty thousand one hundred and twenty-six dollars. I'll give you thirty days to comply."

"Thirty days? You couldn't give me a little more time to secure financing?" Her head spun with the amount of money she'd have to come up with. Even if she sold all her remaining cattle, she wouldn't come close to the amount she needed, and she'd be out of stock, nothing to start over with, nothing to pay the overhead.

"You've had seven years. We sent a payment-due notice in your last statement. I'm really surprised you haven't come in sooner to discuss this matter with me."

He was lying and Mona wasn't buying it. "I never saw it."

Jeffrey Kuhn sat behind his desk, tapping the point of a pen against his date calendar. "Are you having trouble with your mail service as well as cattle rustling?"

"Do you think I'd get *this* upset if I had received the notice? Don't you think I'd have been in here much earlier, had I known?" Granted, she hadn't had time to go through all of what she'd thought was junk mail, but she'd opened and paid her bills. If there had been a note from the bank, she'd have opened it. "Damn it, I know I haven't gotten a single letter from you."

Mr. Kuhn's gray-blond brows rose. "I can't help it if your mail isn't getting to you. The bank stands firm. I'm sorry, Miss Grainger, my hands are tied. Unless you can come up with the payoff amount in thirty days—" he leaned over to look at the desk calendar "—that would be on the twentieth of next month—the Prairie Rock Bank will have to start foreclosure proceedings on the property."

"I'm not believing this."

He shrugged. "I suggest you find another financial institution rather than filing for bankruptcy. You might also consider letting go of some of your help. Like your new hire." He glanced down at his watch, then abruptly stood. "Now, if you'll excuse me, I have another appointment." He cupped her elbow with a cool, clammy palm and urged her from her chair, practically pushing her out the door.

Still too stunned to respond, Mona let him usher her out, stopping only as they emerged in the bank lobby. "Mr. Kuhn…" When she turned to confront her new nemesis, she could have stomped her foot in frustration.

Jeffrey Kuhn had left her standing alone while he smiled and greeted two men wearing expensive suits. With little more than a passing glance her way, Kuhn ushered the wealthier clients through the door of his office, closing it firmly behind them.

Well, that was that. If she needed confirmation that her uncle was right and she was fighting a losing battle, today's news was it.

In a daze, she stumbled out into the Texas sunshine beating the heat into the top of her bare head. She plunked her straw hat in place and stared around the brick-paved Main Street of Prairie Rock, at a loss for what to do. Her feet carried her the two blocks south to Dee's Diner near the town square. She'd left her truck parked near the diner for her lunch date with Catalina, Rosa and Fernando's only daughter.

By the time she pushed through the swinging glass entrance of the café, perspiration beaded on her brow and upper lip and slid down between her pregnancy-enhanced breasts. Since when had walking become more difficult?

Catalina Garcia met her at the door, a mug in one hand and a carafe of aromatic coffee in the other. "Hey, sweetie."

Mona smiled and carefully hugged her friend without spilling the coffee.

"Would you hurry it up? We don't have all day." Wayne Fennel sat at a table several yards away, facing Mona. His shiny new cowboy boots tapped against the linoleum-tiled floor, a scowl marring his otherwise handsome face. The guy had always been a jerk, especially as a football player in high school. Now he owned a body shop with his partner Les Newton, another equally big jerk.

Les turned to stare at Mona, barely giving her more than a glance, but his gaze ran the length of

Catalina's bare legs, a leer forming on his tanned face. A quiet and more creepy version of Wayne.

Mona wanted to throw up. Gentlemen, they weren't. If a barroom fight was what you wanted, you could count on those two to deliver.

Catalina grimaced at Mona and tipped her head toward an empty booth in the far corner. "Take a seat by the window. I'll get you some water just as soon as I take care of Wayne and Les." With a flounce of her long, bleached hair, she hurried toward the two men and sloshed coffee into their mugs.

Catalina had been Mona's friend from the day she was born. They'd been inseparable until their teens when Catalina decided she no longer wanted to be Mexican, Hispanic or anything related to Latino. In the past ten years, Catalina had done everything in her power to change her image from Hispanic to white. From gloriously black to bleached-blond hair, brown eyes gone blue with the aid of contacts, down to erasing every hint of accent from her speech. She even affected a southern drawl around eligible men from the big cities who found their way to the small Texas town.

Not Mona, she embraced everything about her mother's Mexican legacy that she could. It was all she had left of the woman who'd died when she was only six years old.

Mona slid into a vinyl-covered booth overlooking the town square and fought the overwhelming despair washing over her. She wished her mother or father were there to help her figure out the mess she was in. What was she going to do? How could she come up with fifty thousand dollars in a month? She didn't have two nickels to rub together in her savings, having depleted it to pay her hands and make this month's loan payment. The sale of some of her herd was supposed to help her make next month's payment and overhead. Now with over fifty head rustled, even making payroll was looking like a no go.

Catalina swung by the table and called out to the room, "I'm on break, Kelly is covering for me." Then she dropped into the seat across from Mona, her deep-brown brows tugging downward, a sharp contrast to the bright blond of the fringe hanging over her left eye. "What's wrong?"

"Everything." Before she could say more, tears welled in Mona's eyes and spilled over. She brushed them away with the back of her sleeve. "Damn it, I never cry."

"It's the baby talking. All those hormones play hell with a woman's emotions."

"Shh. Don't say that too loud." Mona glanced around the room to see if anyone had heard Catalina's remark.

"Don't worry. I won't tell. Especially since you won't tell me whose it is." Catalina's eyes narrowed. "Was it Jimmy Raye over at Bar M?"

"No. And forget it. I'm not telling anyone. That particular secret will go with me to my grave."

"Damn. And I thought best friends shared all their secrets."

"I can't afford for this one to get out." Mona's gaze dropped to where her hands twisted together, more tears slid down her cheeks.

"Okay, okay. I won't push it. Now tell me what's got your chaps in a twist."

"I just came from the bank." She gulped and forced calm into her voice. "They're going to start foreclosure proceedings on the Rancho Linda if I don't make the balloon payment that's due in thirty days."

"Madre de Dios!" Catalina slammed her palm against the tabletop, all of the Latino in her coming out in the one phrase. "As if you don't have enough problems. Why won't they roll it over into a new mortgage?"

"From what I gathered, they've lost faith in my ability to manage the ranch. What with the rustling and hiring a new ranch hand."

"Was it the advertisement that got them in a froth?" Catalina's chocolate-brown eyes lit. "I have to admit, it reminded me of the Wild West."

Her fit of desperation had backfired, and now Mona regretted placing the ad. However, she didn't regret hiring the man with the gun. His green eyes haunted her thoughts, vaguely familiar, as if she'd seen them before, when she knew she hadn't met him until he'd shown up in the canyon. "Something like that."

"I heard you actually got a man to apply for it."

"I hired one." Mona didn't want to go into the details. She wasn't altogether sure why she'd hired Reed Bryson on the spot. For now, she attributed her brash move to desperation.

"So what's he like? Does he look like Clint Eastwood or John Wayne from one of the old westerns?"

"No. And it doesn't matter what he looks like, I have bigger troubles." She inhaled and let out a deep breath. "How can I come up with fifty thousand dollars in thirty days?"

"Have you tried one of the other banks in Prairie Rock? If they won't help, you may have to go to Amarillo."

"I've never applied for a loan, which means I don't have a credit history. I've only been paying on the loan my father set up." She dropped her head into her hands. "I can't believe I didn't pay closer attention to the terms of the loan. I'm doomed."

"Cut yourself a little slack. It's not as if you've had a lot of spare time on your hands." Catalina snorted. "So who is your cowboy? Anyone I know?"

"Why are you asking? You already know it's Reed Bryson. By now everyone in town should know." She smiled sheepishly.

"I just wanted to hear you say it. So, you hired Reed?" Catalina's brows rose up into the fringe of bangs that swooped to one side of her pale olive forehead. She fanned herself with one of the plastic-coated menus. "He's hot."

"You know him?"

"He broke up a few fights in Leon's Bar over the past couple months while I was working my weekend shift. How could I miss him?" A grin spread across her face. "How'd you catch him? I couldn't get him to ask me out no matter how hard I tried."

"I didn't ask him out, I hired him." Her cheeks warming again, Mona glanced toward the window.

"Your face is turning red. What else did you do? Fess up, girl."

Mona sighed. Her friend knew her too well. "I kinda told Sheriff Lee that Reed and I were living together."

"You did what?" Catalina chuckled. "I'd loved to have been there when you did. That man's been chasing you like a rutting bull for the past few months."

"I know. He doesn't get the meaning of the word *no*. So when he came out about the missing cattle, I made up the story." Mona tried to shrug it off, but Catalina wasn't having any of it.

"And Reed? He went along with it?" Her friend sat back, crossing her arms over her chest. "From what he told me, he didn't want anything to do with relationships. Seems contradictory, if you ask me."

"It was a lie. I made it clear to him that I only wanted him to provide a front to keep the sheriff out of my hair. Nothing else."

"Well, good for you. Maybe something will come of the little game you're playing. You could do worse than have him as a husband."

"I'm not in the market for a husband. I'm looking for a way to save my ranch." Mona stood. "Speaking of which, I need to get moving. The men are out repairing the fences, and I have a loan to secure. Guess I'll check out the competition here and then head to Amarillo."

"What about lunch?" Catalina raced across the floor and grabbed a prepackaged sandwich from a glass-fronted refrigerator. "At least take this."

Although the sandwich looked less than appetizing, Mona accepted it and dug into her purse for money to pay.

"It's on me." Catalina laid her hand over Mona's, halting her search. "You know you'll have to slow down pretty soon, don't you?" She stared at the thickening waist Mona tried so hard to hide by wearing her shirttails loose.

Hiding her bulge wouldn't be an option in the next couple of weeks. She'd be forced to wear bigger shirts and the maternity pants Rosa had purchased from a resale shop. Of all times to be pregnant, now wasn't the best.

Catalina walked with her to the door. "I'd stop by this evening and check out your Mr. Bryson myself, if I didn't have to work. Why don't you bring him by Leon's tonight, if you get a chance."

"Don't think that a smoky bar is the place to be at this time." She ran a hand over her belly, the thought of cigarette smoke making the acid churn.

"I guess not. Then give Reed a kiss for me, will you?" Catalina laughed at the killer look Mona gave her. "Okay, be that way. Keep him all for yourself." She glanced at the white truck pulling into a parking space several yards away. "Look out, there are the Lang Oil speculators from hell."

"Damn." Mona ducked behind Catalina. "Between Teague and Lang, they're as persistent as a heat rash in the summer. Kuhn was pushing Lang as a potential buyer for the Rancho Linda. Not that I'd let that happen. Not as long as I'm still breathing."

Catalina fluffed her bleached-blond hair and smacked her lips together. "Let me take care of them, you can sneak out through the kitchen."

While Mona darted back into the diner, Catalina said, "Hello, gentlemen, come back for some of Dee's apple pie?"

Hurrying through the kitchen, Mona almost slipped on the greasy floor twice before she made it to the back door. But she didn't feel like listening to a sales pitch when she had bigger issues.

With the Lang Oil Exploration people inside Dee's Diner, Mona hurried down the sidewalk to her pickup, shaking her head. Catalina had it all wrong about Reed Bryson. Dating and kissing were at the bottom of Mona's list of things to do when she had a ranch to save.

Then why did Reed's full lips come to mind when Catalina had mentioned kissing?

REED RODE BESIDE Fernando, slowing his horse the closer they came to the broken fence. The other two ranch hands would be here shortly with the pickup and tools to mend the fence.

Last night's search for clues and evidence had yielded nothing. He wanted to go over the area again in the light of day. Assuming the sheriff and his crew of deputies hadn't disturbed the ground too much.

When he was within a hundred yards he reined in his horse. "Let's walk the rest of the way."

Fernando nodded and climbed down from his horse, dropping his reins to the ground. The gelding munched on the prairie grass, his tail twitching like a metronome, swatting at horseflies.

"Miss Mona didn't need this to happen." Fernando stared ahead at the mutilated fence line and off into the distance as though he might spot the missing cattle.

"Does anyone need to be robbed?"

"No, but her being with child makes it twice as hard."

Reed agreed silently. "Any idea who the father is?" He asked the question before he could catch himself. Internally, he rationalized that if the father of the child had a bone to pick with Mona, he could be a suspect in the current situation. What better motive than to ruin Mona Grainger to make her own up to the paternity of her child?

"No. As far as I know, she hasn't told anyone. None of us knew she was even dating." He turned his attention to Reed. "Why did you leave the sheriff's department?"

"I had my reasons." Reed squatted in the dust and stared at the disturbed ground.

"You worked as a police officer in Chicago before that, didn't you?"

That bit of information wasn't hush-hush. Folks in small towns could rarely keep a secret. With a new man in town, word was bound to get around. Especially with a big mouth like Sheriff Parker Lee. "Yeah."

"The Texas panhandle is a long way from Chicago."

In more ways than one. If not for his mother, Reed wouldn't have come back. "I grew up in these parts. Came back because of family."

Fernando nodded. "Family is important."

Some of them.

"Miss Mona swore on her papa's grave she'd keep the land in her family. It meant a lot to him and her mother. She wants to have something to pass down to her child."

"What if her child doesn't want it?" Too often ranches were sold to big corporations when the children showed no interest in eking out a cyclical living on the land. As an only child, Reed had vowed to leave the panhandle rather than work alongside a father who couldn't stand the sight of him. As soon as he'd graduated high school, he'd left, swearing never to return.

Funny how life came full circle and more often than not, he found himself eating his own words. Never say never. As much as he resented his father, Reed couldn't deny his mother anything. When she'd had a stroke, he'd flown home to take turns with his father, sitting by her side in the hospital. When he'd had to leave to go back to Chicago, she'd begged him to stay.

In the end, he'd returned to be closer to her.

Reed shook off the past and focused on the smashed prairie grass all around. "Look here." He pointed at holes in the dirt, spaced evenly in a wide circle. "Looks like they had portable corral panels."

"Sí." Fernando straightened. "They cleaned up well, didn't they?"

"Too well. I don't see tire tracks or hoof prints anywhere around." He stood. All he found were a few footprints probably left by the sheriff's team who'd investigated the site last night.

"As if they raked it before leaving." Fernando crouched next to the loose barbed wire. "Look at this."

Reed joined him for a closer examination. On one of the barbs was a tuft of coal-black human hair and a bloody patch of what looked like scalp. "Someone has a scrape on his head that's pretty deep."

"Sí." The old Mexican nodded farther along in the dust. "They missed a track."

The telltale print of a dog's paw stood out as clear as a signature. Whoever the rustlers were, they had a herd dog. Every rancher on the plains had herd dogs.

An engine's roar alerted him to the approach of a vehicle from the direction of the ranch house.

The ancient red-and-white ranch truck, with the fading sign of Rancho Linda on its side, lumbered across the grasslands, lurching to a stop next to the fence. Chewy, Jesse's border collie, hopped out of the back and ran around the area, sniffing at the tracks.

While Dusty and Jesse unloaded tools from the rear, Reed walked the fence line, bending to inspect the snapped posts.

Dusty dug the blades of a posthole digger in the dirt beside Reed and brushed his gloved hands together. "Won't take long to fix this fence. Jesse and I can handle it, why don't you and Fernando check for any loose steers."

Reed had intended to do just that, but he'd changed his mind. "No. I'll help here, if you don't mind." He stared past Dusty to the foreman.

Fernando nodded and walked across the dirt to his horse, silently climbing into the saddle. He crossed over where the fence should have been and turned to his right. Following the remaining line of wire and posts, he disappeared over a rise.

Reed lifted his hat, brushed the sweat from his brow and grabbed the posthole digger Dusty had left beside him. Ten minutes later, he lifted the last clump of dirt from the hole and set the implement to the side. His muscles burned with the honest effort of physical labor. He hadn't known how much he'd missed it until today.

While he fitted a post into the hole and packed dirt around it, Jesse grabbed the tool and went to work on the next hole, twenty feet away.

Jesse, Dusty and Reed worked at mending the fence. Several wooden posts had been snapped as if run over by something big. Some of the thin metal T-posts had been bent double. Dusty was able to straighten one, but the others snapped off, rust and weather making the metal brittle.

Wielding the posthole digger, Jesse dug through the hard earth, making a hole deep enough for another wooden brace post they'd brought along in the back of the pickup.

The constant sound of metal clanking against metal rang in Reed's ears. Dust kicked up by their heels smelled of Texas and cattle.

Dusty pounded a new T-post in the ground with the heavy post pounder that fit over the post like a giant metal sleeve. He pushed the pounder up and off the post, letting it fall to the ground at his feet. "Going to Leon's tonight, Jess? They're having a wet T-shirt contest, from what I hear."

"No." Jesse raised his arms high and slammed the sharp blades of the posthole digger into the hard-packed dirt.

"Catalina works there tonight. Maybe she'll enter the contest." The sly way Dusty spoke made Reed glance up.

Was Dusty goading Jesse? Did Jesse have a thing

for the pretty young woman he'd seen waiting tables at Leon's?

Jesse's hands paused on the upswing with the posthole digger. "Catalina won't enter." He rammed the diggers into the hole with more force than he'd been using.

"I bet she will. She'd do almost anything for money. Won't she? That Catalina is a wild one." Dusty shot a glance at Jesse. "Wouldn't mind doing the tango with that little chili pepper."

The young Hispanic's face turned a mottled red. "Shut up."

"She's one fine-looking woman."

"Leave her alone." Jesse left the digger in the hole and stalked across the dirt toward Dusty.

A good four inches taller and with twice the bulk as the lean and trim Jesse, Dusty hiked his sleeves up his arms, not a shred of fear in his cocky expression.

"She's better than you."

"She's no better than any of you Mexicans. Except she's a lot prettier. If I want her, I'll take her and there's nothing you can do to stop me."

Red flushed beneath the dark tan of Jesse's skin right before he swung. His fist skimmed past Dusty's jaw as the other man deftly ducked to the left and swung a right hook into Jesse's midsection.

Chewy leaped into the fray, tearing at Dusty's arm, growling like a rabid wolf.

"Damn dog. I'll kill the son of a—" Dusty swung

his arm, pushing the dog out and away from him, the animal slamming against a fence post.

Reed dropped the post he'd been working and grabbed Jesse by the back of the shirt, jerking him out of the path of the bigger man's next uppercut. "Cool it, Dusty."

Chewy staggered to all four feet and shook out his coat before stalking toward Reed now, growling deep in his throat, his gaze sweeping from Dusty to Reed.

Reed nodded toward the animal. "Call off the dog, Jesse."

For a moment Jesse hesitated, then he said in a stern tone, "Down, Chewy."

"Need a bodyguard, Jesse?" Dusty taunted.

"Get out of the way, Bryson." Jesse's voice was low and threatening. "This is between me and the jerk."

"It's over. We have work to do." Reed stood between the two.

Finally, Dusty shrugged and lifted another T-post from the ground at his feet. "Don't know why you get all upset over her. Cat's not all that great. She's got too much attitude for her own good."

"She's got more class in her little finger than you have in your entire body."

"Never said I had class, maybe that's why I like hanging out with her."

"Knock it off." Reed waited a full minute until Jesse went back to work digging his hole and Chewy followed him. The dog planted himself next to the man, his black-eyed gaze following Dusty's every move.

Once Dusty and Jesse seemed in control, Reed went back to the post he'd been working. He kicked dirt into the hole to pack the post in, wishing he could kick a little sense and manners into Dusty. The man was trouble. Why Mona kept him on, he didn't know. Something smooth and black buried in the dust caught the sunlight and glared into Reed's eyes. When he leaned over and brushed aside the dust, he found a square matchbook with white letters spelling out Leon's Bar.

Dusty tossed the pole pounder beside Reed's feet.

Anger bubbled up inside Reed at Dusty's carelessness. The pole pounder wasn't something you tossed close to others. If Reed had moved an inch or two, Dusty could have hit him in the head. The blow from the heavy steel could have killed him or rendered him unconscious with a caved-in skull.

"Find something?" Dusty asked.

Reed's instinct where Dusty was concerned was one of gut-level distrust. He closed his fist around the matchbook and straightened, shooting a glare from the pole pounder to Dusty. "No, I didn't find a thing. Did you?" He moved away from the man, pocketing the matchbook and tucking away a mental note to check out the story on Dusty Gaither.

Chapter Five

Exhausted and dispirited, Mona pulled up in front of the ranch house and shifted into park. All she wanted to do was stand in the shower for twenty minutes and fall into bed. Two hours of sleep the previous night wasn't enough for a pregnant woman.

At five and a half months, she was just beginning to understand her limitations. She hated that she didn't bounce back the way she had before she got pregnant.

Not until she climbed down from the truck did she notice a distinct lack of vehicles around the house and bunkhouse. The only truck was Fernando's lovingly cared for, baby-blue 1967 Chevy pickup.

Before her foot touched the bottom step leading to the porch, Fernando rounded the back of the house. "Miss Mona, you're back."

"I am."

"Any luck with the banks in Amarillo?"

"Not yet. Two agreed to take the application to their underwriters. They'll get back to me sometime next week." She tugged the ponytail loose at the back of her head and shook out her hair. "Where is everyone? Out pulling guard duty?"

"No. We brought the cows in to one of the closer pastures for the night. It was Dusty's night off. Which wasn't a problem until Jesse disappeared after supper. I'd guess they're both headed for Prairie Rock."

"What about the new guy?" Mona avoided Fernando's gaze and saying Reed's name out loud, as though saying it made it more of an intimate question. She sighed. Her sleep-deprived brain was making her loopy. If she wasn't careful, she'd start thinking irrationally and more like a schoolgirl with a crush instead of a savvy landowner. A savvy landowner whose back and feet were killing her.

"Señor Bryson went to town as well."

Mona's head jerked up. "He did?"

"*Sí.*" Fernando crossed his arms over his chest. "I insisted. Since he needed to stop by and visit his *familia* I asked him to go on to Leon's to keep an eye on Dusty and Jesse."

Add a pain in the neck to her list of aching body parts. "So Dusty's been pushing Jesse again?"

"I only caught the end of their argument earlier. I believe it had something to do with my *hija.*"

"*Dios!*" Mona plunked her straw hat back on her head and, ignoring every aching bone in her body and the gnawing hunger in her belly, she marched down the steps and climbed into her truck.

"Miss Mona, Señor Bryson can handle them. My *esposa* has dinner waiting for you. You must think about the *bebé*."

"I'll grab something at Leon's." Mona slammed the door and revved the engine, cutting off Fernando's protests.

Of all the pigheaded male posturing. Dusty couldn't let it go. He knew Jesse was in love with Catalina and she wanted nothing to do with him. Why did he insist on rubbing it in? Too often, his taunting ended in fistfights. Most often when they were at Leon's with Dusty all liquored up.

Darkness cloaked the plains. The scent of dry prairie grass blasted into the open windows of the pickup. The wind helped to keep Mona awake on the thirty-minute drive into Prairie Rock. That and a full-blown, in-your-face desire to slap someone upside the head helped to keep her adrenaline flowing and her eyes open to watch for critters crossing the empty highway.

If she could have fired Dusty, she would have. She couldn't afford to pay her hands much and Dusty hadn't seemed to mind the pittance she could offer him. Reed as well. Until Reed showed up, she thought she'd have to spend the last trimester of her pregnancy on night-watch duty.

Still, she considered letting Dusty go. His redneck attitude had caused more problems than he was worth. Hell, if the bank foreclosed, she'd have to let them all go.

A brick wall of depression played havoc with her emotions and she sniffed several times before she grit her teeth and pressed harder on the gas pedal. She'd be damned if she gave in to her very own pity party.

SITTING IN THE WINDOW overlooking her tiny rose garden, Grace Bryson smiled at her son. The left side of her face didn't respond, but the light in her eyes said it all. "I'm so happy you came to see me. Today, I walked in my garden for fifteen minutes."

Fifteen minutes. This from a woman who'd walked miles of ranchland tending the animals and working alongside her husband to make the spread work for them. Her words were halting and slurred, but she forced them out, like a climber determined to reach the top of a mountain.

As he took his mother's hand, a lump the size of a wadded sock lodged in Reed's throat. "That's great, Mom."

Her fingers curled loosely around his and she gave him a gentle squeeze. "Have you tried talking to your father?"

Reed bent close to hear her words, the slur in her speech making her difficult to understand. She'd come a long way in her recovery from the stroke over the past six months, but the doctor said she might never fully recover her speech.

Reed would take whatever he could get. This woman raised him and loved him unconditionally when his father had shown him little patience or understanding. Why should he talk to his father? They hadn't had anything to say to each other since he'd turned eighteen and left home. "No, I haven't spoken to him."

"He wants to talk to you."

If he'd been so anxious to talk to him, why had he left as soon as Reed arrived? "I'll catch him later. It's getting dark, do you want the light on?"

"Yes, thank you."

He reached above her and tugged the chain for the floor lamp beside her chair.

His mother leaned back against the headrest. "You don't have to wait here with me. William will be back soon. I could stand a little time alone." She chuckled. "I like to take little naps now and then so that I can stay awake through my television shows."

Reed smiled. "Okay. If you're sure you'll be all right."

"I will. Don't forget to talk to your father. He's been meaning to speak with you since you came back. He just doesn't know how."

No kidding. Reed's lips tightened. The only way he'd ever talked to Reed was to tell him everything he was doing wrong. Never a word of encouragement or love.

"Give him a chance. It's not all his fault the way he acted when you were young. If it's anyone's fault, blame me."

He leaned across and kissed her wrinkled forehead. "I couldn't fault you for anything. You were always there for me."

Her grip tightened on his hand and she held him close. "I made mistakes, Reed. Unfortunately, you paid for them."

"I don't understand."

She closed her eyes. "Talk to William. He promised to explain for me." Her grip loosened until her hand dropped from his onto the arm of the lounge chair.

For a long moment, Reed listened for the sound of her breathing. Until he heard her long shallow breaths he didn't breathe himself. Grace Bryson was asleep.

After covering her with a light blanket and tipping the chair to a full recline, he let himself out of the house, locking the door behind him.

He felt strange leaving her alone, but she'd insisted she would be all right. Six months into his mother's recovery, Reed still worried about her. What if she had another stroke?

Darkness had settled in over the town of Prairie Rock. From a distance, he could hear loud country-western music booming into the star-filled night sky. That would be his next stop for the evening. Leon's Bar.

Fernando had insisted he should go to town and play babysitter to the two young hotheads who'd been ready to tear each other's throats out all day. Once off the ranch, with no one to hold them back, they'd probably succeed. Part of Reed was ready to let them go at it. The other part knew Jesse was no match for the much larger and meaner Dusty, and having two of them out of commission would only add more stress. Mona needed ranch hands who could work long, hard days, not men with broken bones, laid up for the next six to eight weeks.

Reed ran a hand down his face. Being up all night had left him tired and cranky. He was used to pulling all-nighters, but they got harder the older he got.

With a sigh, he climbed into his truck and turned toward the bar. He had another reason to come to Leon's Bar—to track a rustler.

When he pulled in front of the ramshackle building made of heavy timbers and corrugated-tin siding, he noted the dozen trucks and cars lining the parking lot. With the band playing a lively tune, the night was just getting started.

Careful not to appear too obvious, he walked in front of the heavy-duty trucks looking for signs of damage from pushing through wooden fence posts. The trucks sporting heavy front grilles all looked as if they'd been driven hard over rough terrain. Any one of them could have done the damage.

At the door, Reed paid the cover charge to a burly man wearing a black cowboy hat and stepped into the smoky tavern. Scantily clad waitresses, wearing shorts no mother should let her daughter out of the house in, sashayed between the tables and bar, filling orders and swatting straying hands.

He spotted Catalina at the bar talking to one of the local ranchers, a tray balanced on one pretty, rounded hip. He could see why Jesse and Dusty were fighting over her.

Her long, blond hair reached down to the middle of her back and her smile and laugh had every red-blooded man in the room turning her way.

Dusty sat at the bar, dressed in clean, pressed jeans and a fancy western shirt with shiny pearl buttons, a sure sign he was on the prowl for a little female company. He shouted for another round of whiskey, his voice loud enough to be heard all the way to the courthouse on Main Street. Definitely loud enough to be heard over the band.

So far, Jesse hadn't made an appearance. Maybe Reed was in luck and he wouldn't have to break up another fight today. One had been enough and he wanted to take the time to people watch. If their black-haired rustler showed up with a cut on his head, he was going to nail him to the nearest post.

Choosing a table as far away from the speakers as possible, Reed sank into a seat in a dark corner, the bass woofer pounding against the inside of his head, even from this distance.

Thankfully, after five more minutes of eardrum-splitting tunes, the band took its first break and the jukebox took over in much lower decibels.

More people drifted in as the hour neared ten. So far Reed hadn't found a dark-haired man with a cut on his head. Then again, most men wore cowboy hats. At least half a dozen had black hair, some long, some short. Reed ruled out the short hair. The length he'd seen on the barb had been at least two inches and straight. Which ruled out the buzz-cut young cowboys two-stepping around the wooden dance floor.

Several Hispanic men crowded around a table at the opposite end of the bar from Reed, all guzzling beer and watching the dancers and other bar patrons.

At least three of the five had longish straight black hair. One had gray hair and the other had his hair cut in a short buzz. Of the three with long hair, two wore cowboy hats.

How to get them out of their hats. Reed bided his time.

"Can I get you another beer?" Catalina Garcia leaned over the empty table next to him and lifted empty bottles onto her tray, a healthy amount of cleavage on display.

"No, thanks." He'd been nursing the same beer since he arrived. It had gone flat and warm, but he wasn't there to drink.

"Mona tells me she hired you out at her place."

"Yes, ma'am."

"Mona's a really nice girl," she said as if commenting on the weather, while she wiped the table with a wet washrag. When she was done, she turned to him. "Don't do anything to hurt her, will you? She's got enough going on in her life."

"She hired me to help her, not hurt her." Reed's brows drew together. "What exactly do you mean?"

The serious look she'd just given him changed into a twisted smile. "You're not exactly hard to look at, you know." With that she flounced away, her bottom twitching back and forth like an open invitation.

An invitation Reed wasn't accepting. Nor was he interested in Mona as anything other than his boss. The end.

"Mind if I join you?"

Reed stiffened. He knew that voice and he'd never welcomed the sound. "As a matter of fact, I do." He didn't turn to look at his father, but a chair scraped and the older man sat next to him anyway.

"I've been trying to talk to you for the past six months, but there never seems to be the right time or place."

"So why bother?" Reed lifted the warm beer and downed the last drops. A long silence stretched between them as the jukebox switched from a lively tune to a cry-in-my-beer song. All the old anger and hurt of his teen years had mellowed into an even stronger indifference for the man who'd never treated him like a son. Now he looked across the table at the weathered, retired rancher, who'd almost lost his wife and immediately afterward sold his ranch. Property that had been in his family for a century. William Bryson wasn't as intimidating as he'd been twenty years ago. He just looked old and tired.

The graying man rested his elbows on the table and laced his fingers. "I'm a stubborn man."

Agreed.

"A stubborn fool," the man continued without looking up. "But one thing is for certain, I've always loved your mother more than anything. It took her almost dying to realize how unfair I've been to you all your life and how hard it was on her."

A lone fiddle picked up the tune on the Jukebox song and played a plaintive melody, accentuating the anguish in his father's voice.

Reed shifted uncomfortably and leaned forward to stand.

"Don't go. I have to get this out. I have a confession to make."

"It's a little late for confessions." Reed continued his upward movement, but his father's hand gripped his forearm and held him.

"It's not just my confession. It's something your mother wanted me to tell you as well. She just doesn't have the strength to right now."

Had it only been his father, Reed would have left. Instead he sat back in his seat. "Go ahead."

"Your mother and I dated for two years before we were married."

"And I was born nine months later. I've heard this story."

"Not quite nine months," he said in a whisper. "What you don't know is that she was pregnant when we got married." His father looked up, his gaze colliding with Reed's. "With another man's baby."

The sound faded into the background of Reed's mind as his father's words sank in. The people moving around the bar blended into a dark blur. "What are you saying? I'm not your son?"

"No." William Bryson stared into Reed's eyes, the lines etched deeply into his weathered face. "And I never gave you a chance to be mine."

Reed shook his head slowly. The way his father behaved toward him all made sense now. The man couldn't love another man's son. His jaw tightened and he leaned toward the man who'd pretended to be his father all these years. "Not that it matters, but who *is* my father?"

"Up until the day I sold the ranch, your mother hadn't said a word. All she told me back when she had her stroke was that she was raped."

The older Bryson's words hit him like a punch to the gut. "Raped? And she didn't tell anyone?" So his father was a scum-of-the-earth bastard. And here he thought the hard, unbending man he'd known as his father was bad. Talk about a winning combination. The heat in the stiflingly full bar got to Reed and he pushed to his feet. "Pardon me."

He couldn't get away from his father fast enough. At first he headed for the door, but then he saw one of the Hispanic men from the far corner getting up and heading for the men's room.

No matter how he felt about his father, he couldn't walk away from the cattle-rustling investigation. He followed the man to the bathroom, hoping to see him without his hat. Perhaps if he only focused on Mona's problems, he could forget his own.

MONA PULLED INTO the parking lot near ten o'clock, tired, disgruntled and ready to kick some ranch hands' butts. And just her luck, Dusty had just shoved Jesse out the front door of Leon's.

Catalina followed on his heels, pounding his back. "Leave him alone, Dusty Gaither, or I'll call the cops!"

In a pool of light cast by the lamp over the door, a crowd of rowdy rednecks gathered around the wrestling men and the one waitress trying ineffectually to break up the fight.

As soon as she opened her truck door, the wind whipped her hair into her face, blinding her for a second. Shouts sounded in between the roaring of the wind in her ears. When she pushed her hair out of her face, and she could see again, fists flew and Catalina was in the middle of it.

"No!" Mona might as well have spit in the wind for all the good her shout did.

"Stop it!" Catalina tried to grab Dusty's arm. He backhanded her and sent her flying into a couple bystanders.

Her blood rushing to her head, Mona tossed her cell phone to the man nearest her. "Call the sheriff."

Then she pushed her way through the thickening crowd, careful to shield her belly from stray elbows.

A roundhouse punch to the gut sent Jesse sprawling in the dirt flat on his back. Mona ran to him while Catalina jumped on Dusty's back.

The cowboy laughed out loud. "That's right, pretty thing. You'll be riding me soon."

When she sank her teeth into his ear, he roared and jerked her over the top of his head, flinging her to the earth.

Jesse stumbled to his feet and charged Dusty.

"Don't go there, Jesse," Mona said in a low, pleading voice. "He's not worth it."

"I'll kill him." Jesse reached out to push her aside.

"Don't or I'll fire you and Dusty both. And where would you get the money to help your mamma?" Mona was running out of steam and her baby was kicking against her ribs so hard, it took her breath away. If she didn't get Jesse to leave soon, she didn't know if she'd still be standing to stop him.

REED RINSED HIS HANDS, taking his time, waiting for the man behind him to finish his business, take off his hat or something.

The dark-haired man flushed and left the bathroom without washing his hands. Reed followed.

A shout went up, "Fight!"

Already people rushed for the door, anxious to see the action.

Like everyone else, the Hispanic man hurried out, his buddies ahead of him.

Reed waded through the crush, two deep behind the disappearing dark-haired man.

When his quarry stepped through the open door, the wind whipped his hat off his head.

No sign of an injury from the back. Reed's pulse quickened and he pushed his way through and out into the open, determined to get around in front of the man.

As soon as he did, he saw it. The angry slash of red high in the man's hairline. This was one of the rustlers. Reed was certain. The man grabbed his hat from the ground and disappeared around the corner of the bar.

Reed took a step toward him, when he heard a shout.

"Go home, Jesse!" The female voice lifted above the heads of the crowd. The determined ring to her tone could be none other than the owner of the Rancho Linda. What the hell was Mona doing here?

Reed shouldered his way to ringside where Dusty and Jesse threw punches at each other. Jesse had a cut high on his left cheekbone, his eye already swelling shut.

A flurry of motion zipped by him and Catalina was kicking, scratching and spitting like a wildcat at Dusty. "Leave him alone, you bastard!"

Reed charged in, jerked Jesse out of the way and stood in front of Dusty. "Catalina, let me handle this."

"Yeah, like you did today?" Dusty waved him

forward with his fists. "Come on. You don't scare me. You want a piece of this, come on."

"I don't want a piece of anything. I want you to go home and sleep it off. Both of you."

"Do as he says, Dusty." Mona stepped up beside Reed.

Dusty crossed his arms over his chest and spit at Reed's boots. "No. I don't have to listen to you and I certainly don't have to listen to a girl who has no business running a ranch."

Reed moved forward, but Mona's hand on his arm kept him from swinging at the man.

"Don't." Mona looked across at Dusty and said in a cool, clear voice. "Don't bother to come back to the Rancho Linda. You're fired."

"You can't fire me. Your daddy hired me."

"Yeah, well, my father is dead, and *I'm* the new owner."

"The hell you are." Dusty lunged at her.

Reed turned sideways and dropped into a ready stance, cocked his leg at the hip and slammed a side kick to Dusty's gut.

The man grunted and staggered backward.

"Don't, Reed. He's not worth it." Mona's hand rested on his arm.

"Get back, Mona, he's not done." As soon as the words left his mouth, Dusty charged again, like a bull in an arena, head down, snorting hot breath through his nose.

Was the guy just stupid? Drawing from within, Reed waited until Dusty was almost on him, then stepped into him, grabbed his arm, walking past him to jerk the arm up and behind him. He applied just enough pressure to make the man hurt, but not enough to break his arm. The point wasn't to damage him, but to make him listen.

"Apologize to Catalina and Mona for being a jerk." Dusty growled.

Reed increased the pressure until the other man was standing on his toes to ease the pain, his growl rising in intensity until he cried out, "Okay! Lighten up."

"What's going on here?" Sheriff Parker Lee, followed by his biggest, meanest deputy, Toby Braxton, shoved his way through the crowd of onlookers.

When Lee saw Reed, he tapped his 9mm pistol in the holster at his side. "Let him go, Bryson."

"Not until he apologizes," he said in a warning tone.

"Let him go, or I'll have to arrest you."

"What for? Dusty started the fight." Catalina got in the sheriff's face. "He's been downright nasty to me and Jesse all night."

"Sheriff, make him stop. He's gonna break my arm," Dusty whined, sounding really pathetic, when a moment before he'd been more than willing to attack a woman.

Reed tightened his grip without raising the man's arm, reminding himself that he was trained in self-

defense not offense. He only went on the offensive when he had no other choice.

"Bryson, you're under arrest for assault." Parker Lee glanced at his deputy and jerked his head. "Cuff him."

Damn it, Dusty wasn't worth the trouble. Reed's gaze caught his boss's outraged look.

Maybe Dusty wasn't worth it, but that beautiful woman with the twin flags of color flying high in her cheeks certainly was.

"I'm not letting go of him until you personally assure me he won't attack Miss Grainger again." Reed's brows rose. "Can you do that? Or is that badge something you picked up in a dime store?"

Sheriff Lee's face flushed a ruddy red in the dim light glowing from the door to Leon's Bar. "Dusty ain't gonna hurt anyone." He pinned Dusty with a glare.

The man had the gall to shrug. "I never attacked her in the first place. I don't know what Bryson's talking about."

"Bull!" Catalina stepped forward. "Ask anyone around. Dusty was the one who started all this."

"I can only go by the facts in front of me." Lee's hand dropped to grip his pistol. "You leave me no choice, Bryson. Let him go, or I'll shoot you."

Chapter Six

Sheriff Parker Lee eased his gun from its holster and aimed it at Reed. The crowd gasped and backed away, leaving a gap behind Dusty and Reed.

Mona's heart fluttered and for a moment, she thought her knees would buckle. Reed Bryson had come to her rescue. He'd been her knight in shining armor when the rest of the world only wanted to watch the fun.

How could she let the sheriff shoot him? Her head swam with the absurdity of it all, like being on the set of a bad western.

"Hey, don't point that thing at me too." Dusty squirmed in Reed's hold. "How do I know you won't miss?"

"I never miss," the sheriff said, his tone low and controlled.

That's what Mona was afraid of.

Reed shook his head, his lips curling in a bitter twist. "Put the gun down, Sheriff, and I'll let him go."

"Fair enough. I'm a reasonable man." He dropped his arm, his finger still on the trigger, even though it was pointed at the ground.

Mona didn't trust him. Something about the hard look in his eyes spelled danger.

Reed shoved Dusty forward and raised his hands. "I'm not armed. You have no reason to shoot."

"You're a black belt in karate. I'd consider that armed." Lee glanced at Braxton. "Cuff him."

The deputy moved forward with the cuffs out in front of him.

Desperation swelled in Mona. She couldn't afford to lose both Dusty and Reed. That would leave only Jesse and Fernando to help her run the six-thousand-acre ranch. Hell, she might as well just help the rustlers load the cattle.

When Deputy Braxton came at Reed with the cuffs, Mona flung herself into Reed's arms. "Oh, thank God you're okay." Then she turned to Parker Lee, whose jaw was twitching on one side. "I'll be pressing charges against Dusty for attacking me, Catalina and Jesse."

"You'll have to do that at the station, after I book Mr. Bryson."

"But you can't arrest him. He was only protecting me and Jesse."

"Just watch me." She held on to Reed's hand, refusing to let the deputy cuff it.

"Move aside or I'll arrest you for obstruction of justice."

"Parker Lee, you wouldn't know justice if it hit you square in the face." Mona's lips pressed into a thin line.

The sheriff held out his own set of cuffs. "Braxton, if she doesn't move, cuff her too."

Reed grasped her shoulders, turning her toward him. He stared into her face, his hands sliding, warm and reassuring, down her arms. "It's okay, baby. I can handle this."

"But he hates me. I should never have involved you in my problems."

"If I didn't want to help, I wouldn't be here." His hands dropped to hers. "Now go home. I'll be there as soon as I can post bail." He set her aside and dug his hand into his pocket.

"Hold it right there." The sheriff's gun was up again and pointed at Reed's chest.

Mona's breath caught in her throat. Was Parker stupid enough to shoot the man with a dozen witnesses standing around?

Reed pulled his hand out of his pocket slowly and held up his truck keys, a tight smile tugging his lips. "Afraid I'll pull my keys on you, Sheriff?"

The crowd of onlookers laughed.

A flush stole under Lee's skin. "You won't need your keys where you're goin'."

"Since the streets of Prairie Rock aren't safe, I'd like Jesse to take my truck back to the Rancho Linda."

"There's nothing wrong with the streets of this town." Sheriff Lee's back stiffened.

Catalina snorted. "Sure as hell is, when the sheriff arrests the wrong man."

Mona agreed with a nod.

Reed held out his wrists to the deputy. "I'm just glad to see the law making the town safe for its citizens. There's nothing like doing what's right and honest by the people who elect you. Is there?"

Braxton slammed the cuffs against Reed's skin.

Though Reed's face didn't change, Mona winced for him. That had to hurt. But Reed wouldn't give the sheriff or his deputy the satisfaction of knowing.

Her heart swelled for a man who'd been a stranger to her yesterday. From what she could see so far, he was decent, honest and stood up for what was right.

Hell, she'd have to fire him.

He didn't belong in the middle of her mess. Never mind, that's what she'd hired him for. Maybe if he were more mercenary, she'd feel better about letting him fight her battles.

Mona sent Jesse back to the ranch and followed the sheriff's car to the county courthouse that also served as the local jail. Her blood pressure boiled over and the baby was kicking up a storm in protest.

After a couple hours of waiting for Reed to be fingerprinted and for the county judge to set bail, Mona posted the amount with the last bit of money left in her checking account.

A few minutes later, the deputy led Reed out of the cell and removed the cuffs.

As Reed passed Parker Lee, the sheriff said in a low, menacing tone, "Stay out of my town, Bryson."

Shocked by his threat, Mona got in his face, wondering what the heck she'd seen in him and regretting ever having dated the man. "It's a free country, Sheriff. You don't own this town."

Instead of responding, he touched a hand to her arm, letting it slide down, skimming her breast. "Do you still scream when you make love?"

Mona raised her hand to slap his face, but Reed captured it in his, halting it before it made contact with the smirk on the sheriff's face.

"Don't ever touch my fiancée again. Do you understand me?"

The sheriff pulled himself up to his full height of just under six feet, three inches shorter than Reed. "Is that a threat?"

"Consider it sound medical advice." Reed raised Mona's hand to his lips and pressed a kiss into her palm. "Come on, sweetheart, it smells rotten in here."

Her heart skipped several beats when his mouth skimmed the overly sensitized inside of her palm. She didn't resist when Reed pulled her against him. Together they walked out of the building.

Past midnight and exhausted beyond coherence, Mona didn't argue when Reed took the keys from her hand. He opened the passenger side of the truck, helping her up and into the seat.

Mona left herself in Reed's hands, laying her head

back against the headrest. *Let him take charge.* All she wanted was to get home, into her pajamas and into her own bed.

"I'll pay back the bail money tomorrow, when I can get to the bank," Reed said once he pulled onto the highway.

"Good, I used my mortgage payment to get you out." Her voice cracked for a moment and then she laughed softly. She couldn't be in worse financial trouble if she'd tried. The bail money was nothing compared to the fifty thousand she had only thirty days to come up with.

"How bad is it?"

"How bad is what? The rustling situation?" Her head tipped to the side so that she could stare across at him. He really was a handsome man, in a rugged, outdoorsy way. "I hired you, didn't I?" She looked back to the truck ceiling. "Speaking of which, you're fired."

"You can't fire me when I'm driving you home."

"You have a point. Then when we get to the house, you're fired."

"Why?"

"You don't belong."

In the light from the dash, she could see him wince and she felt a stab of guilt in her gut. "You don't belong in this crazy, mixed-up mess of politics and thieves. I can handle it on my own." She squeezed her eyes shut at the lie. If she were honest with herself, she'd own up that she was in way over her head and going under for the last count.

"I know how bad the rustling is, how bad off is the ranch?"

"It's none of your concern." She pushed a hand through her hair. "You won't work there after you deliver me to the house."

"Do you stand the chance of losing it?"

Didn't he get it? He was fired. Finished, kaput.

And she'd be finished on the ranch without his help. Mona didn't answer him for a long time, memories of her father riding his favorite buckskin across the range to tend the livestock running through her mind. The few images of her mother were indelibly etched in that ranch house. Would she lose those too if she had to sell?

She closed her eyes to the tears filling them. Who was she kidding? She sighed. "I'd give my right arm to save my home. But I'm not willing to risk others' lives for something I want."

"If it's their choice, why not let them?"

"If something were to happen… Say Jesse was hurt or Fernando or you." She blinked away the tears and stared across the interior of the truck at the perfect stranger she'd just spilled her guts to. "I couldn't live with myself if any of you were hurt because I was too stubborn to give in to the pressure."

"Put it to us and let us make the decision. If we choose to stay, don't feel guilty."

"What about when I can't afford to pay you...?" she asked, her voice fading off.

"We'll cross that bridge when we have to."

"That would be now."

"Why?"

"I found out today that the bank will foreclose on my property if I don't pay the note in full in thirty days." She leaned her head against the back of the seat. Could she be more tired?

"That's why you went to Amarillo?"

"Yes."

"Any luck finding a new lender?"

"No yesses, just maybes." She looked across at him. "Did you guys get the fence up today?"

"Yes, for what it's worth. If the rustlers want to come back, they'll just drive right through it again." He debated telling her the rest and gave in. "We found something today."

Her eyes shot open. "What?"

"A chunk of hair and scalp on the barbed wire, a matchbook and a dog's paw print."

Her gaze returned to the road in front of her, she forced her tired brain to massage the meaning of the clues. "So whoever helped steal my cattle got a nasty cut on his head, smokes and owns a dog?"

"That's pretty much what I figured. The matchbook was from Leon's Bar."

"So that's why you came?"

"I wanted to see if I could find our guy with the

cut scalp. I also came because of some troubles we had on the ranch today. Dusty was itching for a fight with Jesse."

She shook her head. "He used to behave when I was around. I made sure the two weren't together much. Now I won't have to worry about that, will I?"

"What's up with them and Catalina?"

"Dusty knows Jesse has it bad for Catalina and she won't have anything to do with Jesse."

"Why?"

"Did you know Catalina is Fernando's daughter?"

"Fernando and Rosa?"

"That's right. When we were going to high school, Catalina got it into her head that she'd be better off white instead of Hispanic. So she bleached her hair blond and worked hard to erase her Latino heritage, including her boyfriend, Jesse."

"Why?"

"I don't know. Someone must have hurt her feelings pretty bad. I never got the straight story out of her. She wanted out of Prairie Rock as fast as she could get there."

"Did she make it?"

"For a few short months she lived in Dallas. But she couldn't get a decent job with only a high-school education. With housing much more expensive than anything here in Prairie Rock, she couldn't meet the expenses of living in the big city. Before we knew it, she was back. She's taking online courses as she can afford it so that she can get a degree and try it all again."

Reed was quiet for a moment. "I found the man with the cut on his scalp at the bar."

"Who is he?" Mona sat forward, excitement reviving her tired body.

"I don't know. He left the bar about the time the fight started. I would have gone after him, but—"

"—you came to my rescue instead." Mona shook her head. "Did you recognize him?"

"No. He was Latino, needed a haircut and was in his mid-to-late thirties, I'd guess."

"Fernando visits relatives on other ranches and in Prairie Rock. I'll ask him to help us locate him."

"I'm afraid he may be an illegal alien. If that's the case, he won't want to be found."

Mona yawned, her jaw cracking with the force of it. "I'm sorry, that was rude. If I wasn't so exhausted, I'd say let's go back and find our guy." She couldn't even keep her eyes open, how did she think she'd go hunting a thief when she was already half-dead? The baby had taken its toll on her body for the day.

Reed glanced at her, a smile tipping the corners of his mouth. "Go to sleep. I'll get you home safe."

Taking his advice, she leaned back. "You know, you're easy to look at when you smile." Did she really say that? Her mind let the answer trail away. "Thanks for rescuing me tonight," she whispered as she drifted into the blackness of the Texas panhandle prairie.

"THANKS FOR rescuing *me*." Reed knew his words fell on deaf ears, and he was glad of that. He wasn't fully ready to admit that this small woman with the heart of a lion had touched him like no one had been able to in a long time. Perhaps never.

He looked at her again. Dark eyelashes fanned against her high cheekbones. Her black hair lay across her shoulders in thick waves, her belly pushing against the blue chambray shirt she wore, making her appear more plump than pregnant.

Reed found himself wanting to reach out and touch her cheek, her shoulder, her breasts and even the swell of her belly carrying another man's child.

He stared back at the road as a twinge squeezed his chest. A pinch he'd never felt before. "Whose baby is it, Miss Mona?" he whispered into the darkness.

She stirred, her eyes remaining closed. "Can't tell."

Reed couldn't tell if she was really awake when she answered and thought it better not to find out. It was her business, not his.

But why wouldn't she tell? Was she protecting someone? Or was she afraid that someone would take her baby away from her?

Did the father know? Did it matter who it belonged to? Despite her reckless insistence on being in the saddle just as much as any of her hands, she cared about the child growing inside her.

Her hand rested on her stomach, unconsciously protective. Mona Grainger would love her baby no matter who the father was. Just like his mother. Even if it meant keeping the secret of its lineage from everyone, including the father and the baby.

The world lumped into Reed's gut. If she married, would she take care to choose a man who'd love the child no matter what, or would the kid go through life wondering what the hell he'd done to his father to make him hate him so much?

What did Reed care? He probably wouldn't stay around long enough to find out. Once he resolved the rustling situation, he'd have to find another job. Maybe he'd go back to Chicago. His father—no, stepfather—could care less about him. When he came back to the panhandle, he'd come to see his mother and she was improving daily. If he left, she'd be well cared for by his stepfather. A fact he'd had to accept, despite his own interactions with the man so many years ago.

Reed glanced back at Mona. Like his mother, she'd apparently fallen in with the consequences of the wrong man, got knocked up and had to live with her actions. His mother had suffered through Reed's childhood, always playing mediator between him and his father. He'd seen the pain in her eyes, knew how much it hurt her that the two men in her life couldn't get along. Would Mona be the same?

The woman already struggled with a big enough burden handling a ranch on her own. The right husband could help her with the daily operations, but could he help her with raising a child?

The porch light served as a beacon in the sea of dark prairie grass. He hadn't realized how tired he was until he pulled into the driveway.

Mona had slid to the side, her head resting on his shoulder. When he turned off the engine, she didn't awaken. Instead, she snuggled closer, pressing her cheek against his chest. He touched a hand to her shoulder and shook her.

The poor woman was so tired, his shaking had no effect on her.

However, his hand on her arm was having an effect on him. Mona Grainger was warm, soft and…and entirely too trusting. His thoughts veered into inappropriate waters for an employee. Maybe she was right, and he should leave.

Reed struggled between shouting to wake her and leaving her to sleep in the truck. Finally, he scooted her across the bench seat, lifted her into his arms and carried her into the house.

Walking past his assigned room, he stepped into the master bedroom with the king-size four-poster bed, draped in a solid white, fluffy comforter. When he laid her down, he stepped back with every intention of leaving the room as quickly as possible.

But she still wore her boots. He couldn't leave her to sleep in her dirty boots on that white bed.

If he were smart he would. But he hadn't been

very smart where Mona Grainger was concerned. If he had, he'd never have agreed to take the job in the first place.

Lifting one leg, he eased off her boot and sock, marveling at how delicate her foot was, the fine bones surely too fragile to carry her about all day long, riding, roping and dealing with redneck cowboys. Her shirt had crept up, exposing the jeans she wore unbuttoned and half unzipped to allow for the slowly expanding belly, now a smooth curve.

Reed was familiar with pregnant women from his time working for the Chicago police. Once, he'd come close to having to deliver a baby in the back seat of a taxi cab. Thankfully, the Emergency Medical Services arrived in time to do the job.

But he remembered the joy of watching that baby being born. The miracle of life in the making and the love the woman had for a little person she'd held in her arms for the first time that day. What would it be like to watch the birthing of Mona's baby? Would she have someone with her when the time came?

"I'll take care of her, *señor,*" a voice said from behind him.

Reed spun, caught in the act of staring at the boss as she slept.

Rosa Garcia smiled. "She's an angel, isn't she?"

Had she read his mind? Could she see he'd been thinking the same thing, longing to touch Mona's soft cheek, the swell of her breasts and the curve of her hips? With heat rising up his throat, Reed dropped the sock he'd been holding and laid Mona's leg softly on the bed.

Tomorrow, after a good night's rest, he'd pack his bags and leave.

Chapter Seven

"I thought I fired you." Mona entered the barn to find Reed brushing her horse.

When she crossed to where her saddle lay across a saddle tree, he made it there before her.

"You need to quit lifting heavy objects." He carried the saddle and a blanket to the horse and tossed them on its back.

"Hey, I'm the boss. I give the orders around here." For a moment she'd bristled at his high-handedness, but then she'd recognized that he was only trying to protect her and her baby. That made her feel entirely too warm and fuzzy inside. Not a good sensation when you're trying to establish yourself as a ranch owner capable of doing anything a man can do.

Okay, so she was almost six months pregnant and her doctor had told her to slow down, saying pretty much the same thing Reed had. She wasn't supposed to lift anything over twenty pounds.

Rather than argue with the help, she chose to be

thankful. She did insist on tightening her own girth and bridling the mare herself. "Where's Jesse?"

"Rosa had him down with an icepack on that eye. It was swollen shut this morning."

"I should have fired Dusty a long time ago. He's always been cocky and looking for trouble. More so since my father died. He didn't think a woman could run this ranch." She shrugged. "Maybe he was right."

"I'm not sure anyone could do any better under the circumstances. Shorthanded, cattle rustling and…" He nodded toward her belly.

She laughed. "I'm doomed, aren't I?"

"I wouldn't say that. The odds are stacked against you right now, but that could change." His gaze captured hers. "I'll do my best to make it change."

Deep down, she knew he meant every word and it gave her comfort she hadn't felt in weeks. A flicker of hope sprang in her chest. With Reed helping her, she could conquer anything. She'd just have to remind herself, he wasn't permanent. No man was.

He was nothing more that hired help, loading a saddlebag with a come-along, hammer, nails and a coil of barbed wire. He knew what needed to be done and he did it. No prodding necessary.

They rode in silence, checking the perimeter fences with a few stops along the way for her to find a lone bush to pee behind. The treeless Texas prairie wasn't the best place for a pregnant woman to find relief. But it couldn't be helped and Reed was considerate, giving her the necessary privacy.

Mona didn't have anyone else to do the work, so she needed Reed to help her. The weather had been dry lately and the herd couldn't be kept locked up long in the smaller pasture close to the house. They'd shear the grass to a nub in a day and she couldn't afford to feed them baled hay or grain. Hell, she could barely afford groceries for the hired hands and the house, much less the animals.

"See that?" Reed nodded ahead.

They'd made it all the way around to the north pasture, the one she'd planned on turning the cattle loose in as soon as possible. It was also the most vulnerable, being next to a gravel county road. A broad tangle of barbed wire lay on the ground, leaving a gaping hole in the fence.

Reed dismounted and reached up to help Mona down.

"Thanks, but I can do it myself."

He shrugged and stepped back. "Suit yourself."

After Mona swung her leg over the horse, hands reached up to help her the rest of the way to the ground. Firm but gentle hands.

An electric shock ran from where his hands rested on her hips, all the way through her body. How could a woman who was almost six months pregnant and whose body was bulky and misshapen feel desire for a stranger? But she did. An over-whelming urge to feel his hands on her naked skin washed across her, making her nerves tingle with awareness.

As her feet touched the ground, she let herself lean into him, inhaling the scent of leather and prairie on his skin. So earthy and fresh, not coated in cologne and filled with lies.

"See these?" He released her and squatted on the ground beside the barbed wire. He pointed at grooves in the ground from knobby tires. "Four-wheeler tracks. Looks like they originate from the county road and go into your property, what I would guess to be a long way. If you want, I could follow them."

"Not necessary. They were fishing for cattle and didn't find any within easy range."

"Good thing Fernando had them penned closer to the house."

"Yeah." Her chest tightened. "I can't keep this up. Either I lose cattle to thieves or lose them to starva-tion." Her eyes stung with mounting moisture. "Damn it." She brushed at a tear, only more fell in a slow, steady stream. She used the back of her blue chambray sleeve and wiped at the tears until she soaked her sleeve. "I'm sorry. I can't seem to stop."

Reed straightened and dug into his back pocket, unearthing a red bandanna. "Let me." As careful as a surgeon, he dabbed at her eyes, plucking the loose strands of hair off her wet cheeks and pushing them behind her ear. "Better?"

Mona sniffed, more tears trickling down her face. "Why are you being nice to me?"

"It's all part of the cowboy-to-the-rescue job. Didn't you read my résumé?"

She laughed, then hiccupped and snatched the bandanna from him, her fingers colliding with his for longer than necessary. "Actually, no. You never gave me one."

"What kind of boss are you? You should always check out a man's references before hiring him. You never know when he might be a fugitive, running away from the law." He raised her hand to capture yet another tear with the bandanna she clutched.

"Are you?"

"A fugitive?" His hand fell to his side, his gaze never leaving her.

"Not running away from something or someone?"

Reed stared at her for a long time, and then turned toward his saddlebag. "No."

Had she struck a chord that hurt?

He didn't give her a chance to ask further questions. Instead, he went to work attaching a strand of the wire he'd brought to the cut wire to make it longer. Then he hooked the come-along around a fence post and tied the wire to the end.

"Stand back in case the wire snaps."

Chafing a bit at his demands, Mona stepped back.

This was work she could do with her eyes closed. But he was right. If the wire snapped, she could injure her baby as well as herself.

While Reed worked each of the four wires, Mona handed him supplies, making sure she moved away when it came to stretching the wire taut. But she had plenty of time to watch him, her mouth growing dry as he bent, flexed and strained his muscles.

"Could you hand me the hammer?" He held out his hand. "And tell me why you jumped into the middle of last night's fight?"

She stared at him a moment, letting the questions sink in, taken aback by the second one. She grabbed the hammer from his saddlebag and laid it in his out-stretched palm a little harder than necessary. "I had to. Dusty would have killed Jesse."

"He could have killed you and your baby as well." He cranked the come-along until the bottom strand of barbed wire stretched tight. Then he positioned the horseshoe-shaped nail over the wire and hammered it into the post.

Even after he'd hammered the second nail in, Mona didn't have a response for him. He was right. Almost six months pregnant wasn't the stage at which a woman should be jumping into a fight. But he didn't have to point it out to her, she knew it. That he was right made her mad. "Is this your idea of casual conversation?"

He straightened and walked to where she stood beside his horse.

The closer he came, the less air entered her lungs until she breathed in shallow breaths, her body alert and ready. For what?

He stopped with his toes almost touching hers, then he leaned toward her, as if he would kiss her. "Are you bent on losing that baby?" He reached out his hand, skimming past her shoulder to snag the wire cutters from his saddlebag. His mouth brushed close to her ear, but he returned to the fence without laying one lip on her.

He might as well have. Mona labored to inhale and exhale at a normal rate and her blood raced through her veins. Damn the man. He had to know his effect on her, or why tease her like he'd just done? "Why did you quit the sheriff's department?" There, that ought to cool his heels.

Her question made him pause while tying another strand of barbed wire to the next cut piece of wire. "Did you know Tyler Jones?" He wrapped the wire, using more force than necessary.

She shook her head. "I didn't know him personally, but I'd heard about his accident. Such a shame. He was so young. Twenty-four, right?"

"Twenty-four, with a brand-new baby and a young wife." He hooked the come-along to the second wire and cranked it several notches. "Despite what the newspaper said, he didn't have an accident. He was run off the road while out investigating a call from someone who'd called in a suspected cattle rustling.

The sheriff sent him out there alone, no backup. It was my night off, but I heard the call over my home scanner." Reed cranked the wire tighter, his lips set in a thin line. "I called the sheriff and told him Tyler needed backup. When he refused to send it, I offered to go myself. The sheriff ordered me to stand down. I refused the order. I found Tyler's car. I was the one who told his wife. She just held her baby and cried."

"I didn't know."

"Parker Lee knew better."

"So you quit?"

"I couldn't work for a man who didn't care enough about the people who work with him."

Mona nodded. "What keeps you here?"

"I came back to the panhandle to be close to my mother after she'd had a stroke."

Mona's heart squeezed. "I can understand. I wish I'd had more time with my mother and father. Is your father still alive?"

Reed didn't answer.

After a minute passed, Mona got the message. "I'm sorry. I take it he is and you two don't talk much."

"I recently learned the man I thought was my father was only my stepfather and not a very good one at that."

"And you don't know who your father is?" Her breath caught in her throat. "Your mother never told you." Mona turned away, grabbing for the bandanna she'd stuffed in her back pocket before the tears fell.

She couldn't tell anyone who the father of her baby was. The stakes were too high.

What had been Reed's mother's reason? Only a mother determined to protect her baby would keep a secret for so many years.

"No, my mother never told me. She let me believe my stepfather was my real father until last night."

Mona spun to face him. "I'm sorry."

"Actually it was a relief. For years, I thought he couldn't love me because of something I did. But it wasn't because of what I did, but who I was."

Mona crossed over to where Reed stood and laid her hand on his arm, feeling awkward but wanting him to know she cared. "It must have been tough to hear something like that."

He grabbed her wrist and held it away from him. "Will you lie to your child?"

"I'll do whatever it takes to protect my baby. No one will know who the father is, including the child. At least until he or she is grown and can understand my reasons."

He stared at her a long time before he let her go. "It's your business."

She rubbed her wrist and put distance between them. Yeah, it was her business, and Reed wasn't. She'd do well to remember that.

WHAT HAD COME over him? Mona wasn't his mother. For that matter, he didn't know the reasons his mother had kept her secret. Many women who'd been raped didn't tell because of the shame they felt. Had his mother felt too ashamed to go to the police? Or had his father been someone of influence who could have hurt her more or taken her baby away from him.

Had Mona been raped like his mother? Was that why she was afraid to say anything?

A quick glance at the woman willing to face a herd of wild boars gave him his answer. No, shame wasn't it. If she'd been raped, she'd have gone to the nearest law enforcement agency and told them.

Then again, she seemed as aware of Parker Lee's shortcomings as a law enforcement official as he was. Whatever her reason for keeping her secret, as he'd told her, was her business.

Reed hammered another nail into the fence post and moved on to the next wire, stretching it taut. He ratcheted the come-along, testing the tightness with each click of the crank.

On his last crank, the wire snapped at the other end. "Get back!" he yelled and dived for the side, but too late. All he could do was fling himself to the ground, cover his face and hope for the best. Because his end was still tied to the come-along, the long strand contracted like an accordion, whipping back toward Reed.

"Reed!" Mona screamed.

Metal spikes pierced his skin, tearing through his jeans, shirt and scalp.

"Stay back until it stops bouncing." With his head covered, he couldn't see if she was doing as he asked. He could only hope she was. Being wrapped in barbed wire was no picnic. It hurt like hell.

When the wire quit vibrating, Reed tried to move. Even the slightest movement made the barbs dig deeper into some area of his body.

"Stay completely still. I've got the wire cutters. I'll get you out." Although her voice shook, he could tell she was trying to keep him calm.

"Trust me, I'm not going anywhere until this stuff is cut off. But not by you. Leave me here and go get Fernando. I don't want you getting tangled up in this mess as well."

"It's okay. I know what I'm doing." A snipping sound was accompanied by a strand of the barbed wire loosening its sharp grip on his shoulder. Another snip and she lifted away the strand piercing his scalp.

"Thanks, that one was hurting."

"And bleeding." She touched something to his head.

"We can fix the blood later."

"Right." She went back to work, cutting one strand at a time until he was free.

When she removed the last strand from the back of his thigh, Mona sat back in the dirt, sweat sliding down the side of her face. "There. You can move now."

Reed sat up, wincing. "Now I know what my dog felt like after his losing battle with a porcupine."

"You have a few cuts here and there, but you'll live. Come on, let's get you back to the ranch house."

"Not until I get this fence finished."

"No way. Those barbs were rusty. When was your last tetanus shot?"

"Less than a year ago."

"Good thing. Still, you can get infections from puncture wounds."

"We'll leave when I finish this fence." He made her wait until he had the last two strands nailed in place.

Only then did he consider heading back to the house. He'd inspected the other end of the wire that had wrapped around him. Someone had cut it deliberately. Not all four of the strands, just the one. As though setting it up to snap when stretched tight.

Anger, edged by dread, shot heat throughout his body. What if Mona had been tightening that wire? What if he'd listened to her and left when she'd said he was fired? She'd have been alone, trapped in the wire.

No, Fernando would have gone with her. He would have pulled her free.

Still, despite the pain and sting of all the puncture wounds on his body, he was glad he was the one who'd been injured, not Mona.

When they arrived at the house, it was empty, with a note on the counter from Rosa and Fernando. Fernando had gone with Rosa to buy supplies. They'd be back after dinner with Catalina.

"You can be first in the shower. I have a call to

make." He eased his cowboy hat off his head,
wincing when the dried blood in his hair stuck to his
hat for a second.

"Are you sure? You should get yours first. You
look terrible."

He smiled. "Thanks."

"No, really. The sooner you're clean, the better
I'll feel."

"I have to make a call first," he repeated. "Go on."
He shooed her toward her bedroom and headed for
the phone, hoping he'd be able to get in touch with
a friend of his in Chicago. He had a favor to ask.

MONA HURRIED through her shower, being careful
not to use all the hot water. Reed had been good
about her cutting away all the barbed wire, but he had
to be hurting still.

With her hair wrapped in a towel, wearing nothing
but shorts and a cotton blouse half buttoned and tied
loosely over the bump at her waist, Mona hustled out
of the shower. "Your turn," she shouted, shutting the
door to her bedroom behind her.

After swiping a brush through her tangled hair, she
checked her face and clothes. Because the air conditioner wasn't keeping up with the heat outside, Mona
had chosen shorts. Were they too revealing? With
Rosa and Fernando out of the house for the evening,
Mona was alone with Reed. Alone and facing duties
normally performed by Rosa—cooking and tending

to wounds. Two things Mona had relied on Rosa to do all her life. Where did she start? "Band-Aids and ointment." She'd worry about food later. Maybe a can of soup and grilled-cheese sandwiches?

Mona rifled through the first-aid kit located in the kitchen, scrounging a tube of antibiotic cream and a full box of Band-Aids. He'd need the whole thing with the number of holes he had in his body.

The longer he took, the more agitated Mona became. She tugged a skillet and a can of soup out of the cabinet. What was taking him so long? A quick glance at the clock and her face burned. Five minutes had passed. Okay, so she wasn't anxious to apply the cream to his wounds. Or was she?

Blood rushed from her head to her belly and lower, making her hot in places she hadn't been since she'd found out she was pregnant. The blouse she wore had been loose until her boobs had grown. Now her nipples puckered and pressed against the white cotton. They might as well be neon blinking lights. On her way back to her bedroom to change, the bathroom door opened and Reed stepped into her path.

She'd been hell-bent on changing and didn't see the door open or Reed step out until she ran headfirst into his broad, naked chest.

Her nose smashed against the coarse blond hairs scattered across his bronzed chest. The man must have gone shirtless a lot to be that tanned. He smelled of soap and man. And he was wearing stretchy gray gym shorts, displaying thickly muscled thighs, slightly lighter than his chest, but still tanned and gorgeous.

Mona's knees melted and she almost collapsed in a puddle in front of him, if he hadn't grasped her arms and held tight. "Oh, you're done." Ranch owner to blithering idiot in ten seconds flat.

A smile curled his lips. "I can be quick when it hurts."

At the mention of pain, Mona snapped out of her stupor and spun around. "Oh yes. I have Band-Aids and ointment in the kitchen for you. Why don't you lie down on your bed. I'll be there in just a minute."

Reed followed her until he reached the doorway to his room, where he stopped. Mona continued to the kitchen.

With him behind her, Mona wondered what he thought of seeing so much of her legs. She'd been in jeans every time she'd seen him before. As conspicuous as she felt, she might as well have been naked.

Armed with the tube of antibiotic ointment and Band-Aids, she returned to his room.

Reed stood beside the window, staring out at the sunset.

She steeled herself to act impersonal and businesslike, when all she wanted to do was drool. "Lie down on the bed on your stomach." While he complied, she turned her back, retraining her body in the necessary art of breathing. What was wrong with her? Had he been Jesse or Fernando, she wouldn't hesitate for a second. Nor would she be breathing as though she'd been running for the past fifteen minutes. If she were honest with herself, she'd recognize the fear, apprehension and unquenchable desire, all raging within her. Her body was on fire!

Boy, she was in over her head. To keep from flapping her hands, she grabbed the ointment and unscrewed the top. "Where shall I start?" When she finally looked at him, he was lying on his side smiling up at her.

"You don't have to do this." Reed held out his hand. "Give me the ointment, I can do it myself."

That smile rankled her. Did he think she couldn't do the job, couldn't remain impartial in the application of first-aid on one of her men? "No, you can't reach the middle of your back. If Rosa were here, she'd do it. Since she's not, it's up to me." She moved closer to the bed, her breath coming in short gasps. His back was every bit as yummy as his front. Broad shoulders, rippled with muscles, the skin tanned a nut brown. With a dab of ointment on the tip of her finger, she touched it to the first puncture wound.

The muscles of his back contracted and he shivered.

"I'm sorry, did that hurt?" She touched his arm with her other hand.

"No, just get it done." His words were tight, as though he'd said them with teeth clenched.

She must have hurt him. At the next wound on his shoulders, she dabbed gently and carefully rubbed the cream into the wound, using a slow circular motion. His skin heated beneath her fingertips and she widened her motion to include the full expanse of his right shoulder.

His skin stretched tightly over muscles as hard as steel. When she moved to the other side, the story was the same. The man obviously worked out. No man could have muscles that big without making the effort to use them. Hell, he'd lifted her on more than one occasion without any effort whatsoever. His arms had been like steel bands holding her steady.

Her hands moved lower, massaging the ointment into the puncture holes around his lower back. Mona tugged her shirt away from her breasts, the fabric sticking to her skin. Was the air conditioner working at all?

"I could wait until Rosa gets back."

"No. She'll be tired and by then, infection might have set in. Did the barbed wire go through your jeans?" Her hand hovered over the elastic band of his shorts, her mind going blank beyond wanting to move the shorts lower.

Reed rolled to the side and grabbed her wrist. "I'll take care of the rest." He sat up, swinging his knees over the side of the bed. Still he didn't let go of her hand.

"Are you sure?" Her lips were so dry, she ran her tongue across them.

"What are you doing, Mona?" His grip tightened, drawing her closer until she stood between his naked knees, skin touching skin.

"I thought you knew." Mona's head spun, her heart beating too fast. What was she doing? Her gaze locked in on his lips and she swayed toward him.

Reed dropped her hand, captured her hip and dragged her against his chest. His fingers dug into her thick, damp hair, winding around a heavy strand. "This won't solve your problems, but damned if I can resist." Then his lips descended on hers, at first crushing them, his tongue pushing past her teeth to tangle with hers.

He tasted of mint and smelled of soap, a fresh combination, completely sexy. Mona sank against him, her bottom finding purchase on his thigh.

With a gentle twist he had her lying beside him on the mattress.

Her arms circled his neck, bringing those incredible lips back to hers. Mona could die this way and be happy.

Reed's hand smoothed across her collarbone and down to the first button on her cotton shirt. With a flick of his fingers, that one loosened, exposing more of her breasts.

The juncture of her thighs tingled deliciously. She wanted him more than she'd wanted any man. And though she knew she shouldn't, she couldn't stop herself.

The next two buttons came undone, the knot the only thing keeping the blouse from gaping open.

Mona's hands rose to remove the knot, but Reed

brushed them aside. He bent to touch his lips to her throat, blazing a trail down her neck and lower to the valley between her breasts.

His fingers removed the knot, spreading her shirt wide enough he could stare down at her.

A burst of panic overcame her. He'd see her body for what it was. Pregnant and unappealing. Breasts too large, the lump of her baby protruding as a reminder she'd been with another man. Tiny stretch marks marring her skin.

Mona laid still, her breath caught in her throat, those dratted tears threatening to fall.

Reed's hand lifted to cup one breast, massaging the tip to a hard little nub. His mouth descended on the other, drawing it between his lips and teasing it with his tongue until Mona arched off the bed, pushing closer to him.

Her fears evaporated momentarily in the ecstasy of his touch, until his hand slipped lower to the gentle slope of her belly.

Mona reached up and captured his fingers in hers. Her brain reengaging, reason flooding back, shoving aside the blinding web of desire. "No. I can't. I shouldn't." With a sob rising in her throat, Mona scrambled off the bed and ran out of the room.

Alone in her room with door locked, she let the tears fall unchecked. She knew what she'd been feeling, but what had she been thinking? He was the hired help. She was an unmarried ranch owner on the verge of losing everything. She sank to the edge of the bed and buried her head in her hands, silent sobs racking her body.

"Mona?" Reed called out to her through the wood-paneled door.

Mona buried her head under her pillow to shut out the sound. She couldn't go to him. He was her employee, not her lifeline. She'd made her bed nearly six months ago, choosing to believe in a man unworthy of her affection. It was her mistake to live with. Not that her child would ever feel like a mistake. But the father would never know, if she could help it.

And Reed deserved a woman who didn't have so many strikes against her.

The long day and even longer bout with tears, something she didn't indulge in often, took their toll on Mona and she fell asleep.

Not until the fifth ring did she hear the phone through the thickness of her pillow. By then it stopped ringing. The blue numbers on her digital alarm clock indicated 11:38. Who would call that late?

The next thing she knew, her door was being attacked by a jackhammer. The banging was so loud, the baby kicked a protest against her ribs.

"I'm coming." With a hand over her belly to calm her child, she hurried to the door and yanked it open.

Reed stood in front of her, fully dressed in jeans, shirt and boots. "Get some clothes on. Catalina's been taken to the hospital in Amarillo."

Chapter Eight

"What happened?" Mona slid into the passenger seat of Reed's truck.

"Fernando and Rosa got the call on their cell phone as they left a friend's house in Prairie Rock. All they knew was that the bartender at Leon's found Catalina unconscious in back of the bar."

Mona's stomach roiled. "Do you think it was Dusty?"

"I don't know. I'm hoping Catalina can tell us once we get there."

"I hope she's all right." Mona slammed her fist against the door panel. "Damn it! She has to be."

Reed drove the hour it took to get to the hospital in Amarillo, trying not to glance at Mona every five minutes.

She looked so small and vulnerable sitting up straight in the seat next to him. Her eyes were puffy and red-rimmed, as if she'd been crying.

He could have kicked himself for kissing her.

Before, they'd maintained a professional distance and she'd been more or less accepting of his help. Now, that was shattered.

She didn't need more complications added to her life and he certainly wasn't the right man to complicate it. He took a deep breath and let it out, amazed at how tense he was. "I'm sorry. I shouldn't have come on to you."

"Seems I was the one coming on to you." She sighed. "Let's forget about it."

"If you fire me, I'll understand and leave." Not that he wanted to leave. On the contrary, with too many unanswered questions and thieves out there preying on one overstressed, pregnant cattle rancher, he'd feel as if he'd failed in his duty if he did go.

She shoved a hand through her hair, her lips lifting in a crooked smile. "I fired you before, you didn't leave."

The smile, no matter how weak, gave him hope. "If you want me to leave, this time I'll respect your wishes." *And find some other way to help.*

She sat still, with her gaze pinned to the road, her fingers twisting in her lap. When she spoke, her words were strong, resolute. "You can't leave. I don't have anyone else."

Alone. This brave young woman was pregnant and alone against the world. Despite her condition, she willingly took on the challenge to keep what was hers and what she wanted to share with her child. She had more grit than anyone Reed knew. Mona wouldn't give up the fight.

Reed's heart swelled behind his ribs. He completed the remainder of the trip in silence, afraid he'd say something stupid or sentimental if he opened his mouth.

Before he cut off the engine in the parking lot, Mona was on the ground and hurrying toward the emergency-room entrance of the hospital. A quick stop to ask directions and they were on their way up in the elevator, silence stretching between them. They found Fernando and Rosa hovering around one of the two beds in the hospital room. As soon as Mona walked through the door, Rosa fell into her arms, sobbing and speaking Spanish so fast, Reed couldn't keep up. He understood a little of the language, but not enough to catch what the frightened woman said.

Fernando held out his hand to Reed. "*Muchas gracias,* Señor Bryson. Thank you for coming."

Reed took the older man's hand and shook it, his gaze going to Catalina. Her bleach-blond hair lay tangled against the sheets. A nasty cut grazed her right cheekbone, a deep purple bruise just beginning to show through her skin. Her bottom lip was swollen and cracked, dried blood clinging to the damage.

"Has she been awake?" he asked.

"No. She's been unconscious since we got here. She had a blow to the back of her head and a few cuts and bruises to other parts of her body." Fernando's fists clenched and unclenched. "Someone beat her."

Rosa grasped her daughter's hand and lifted it to her lips, tears streaming down her face. "Catalina, *mi corazón.*"

Mona ran her hand down Catalina's arm. "Who would do this?" Her eyes widened and she looked to Fernando. "Was she…?"

The older man shook his head. "The doctor checked. There weren't any signs of rape." He touched a hand to his daughter's leg, buried beneath the white hospital blanket. "We won't know who did this until Catalina can tell us."

"Go home, *hija.*" Rosa wiped her tears away and stared across her daughter's inert form to Mona. "There's nothing more to do but wait."

Facing Mona, Reed waited for her decision. Personally, he wanted to be there when Catalina regained consciousness. The sooner they discovered who her attacker was, the better.

"I'm staying here with you." She looked across at Reed. "Do you think Jesse will be all right at the ranch by himself?"

Reed nodded. "He's armed to the teeth and by now, sitting out in the pasture singing to the cattle."

Catalina stirred and mumbled something.

"*Sí*, Catalina?" Rosa bent closer.

"Jesse can't sing," she said, her voice strong enough for Reed to hear across the room.

Mona chuckled, dropping a kiss to her friend's uninjured cheek. "You're right. But those cows are tone deaf. They actually like to hear him sing."

"Mamá? Papá?" Catalina blinked up at her mother and father. "I'm sorry."

She smoothed the hair away from her daughter's face. "For what, *hija*?"

"Everything." She sighed and closed her eyes.

"Catalina, who did this to you?" Mona asked.

The loving way she spoke touched Reed in a way he didn't think possible. These people were her family. Blood didn't matter, the heart did.

For a long moment the battered woman didn't answer.

Reed assumed she'd fallen asleep or was unconscious again.

"I don't know," she whispered. "I didn't see their faces."

"Did you hear them?" Her father lifted her hand. "Did you recognize the voices?"

"I don't know. I wait on so many at the diner and the bar." She inhaled and let out the breath in a long slow exhale. "Mona, they weren't Latino."

"How do you know that?" Reed asked.

"No accent and their hands were white. I think one had blue eyes." Her eyelids fluttered open and she stared up at the ceiling. "Yes, I saw blue eyes as I passed out. I can't remember anything else."

"Any idea why they attacked you?"

"Oh yes, I know why." Her lip turned up in a snarl. "The bastards were talking about stealing more cattle. I overheard them talking out behind Leon's Bar. After dinner with *Mamá* and *Papá* I went to work at Leon's. I entered through the back door, since I didn't want Leon to know how late I was. It must have been after ten." She paused for a few shallow breaths, wincing when her rib cage moved. "They were around the other side of the building from where I was. When I heard voices, I moved closer to see who it was. They stood in the shadows, so I couldn't see their faces. I must have made a noise, because they stopped talking and turned in my direction. I knew I was in trouble, so I ran for the door." She sighed. "They caught me before I got there. Oh, Mama, I thought they were going to kill me. And they would have if I hadn't pretended to be dead."

Mona squeezed Catalina's hand. "You're okay now, *mi hermana.*" My sister.

"Mona." Her hand gripped Mona's and she looked up into her eyes, a glaze of pain dulling the natural deep brown irises. "They were talking about the Rancho Linda. They were planning another hit on your ranch."

Her lips thinning into a straight line, Mona gripped Catalina's hand tighter. "Did they say when?"

"I didn't hear that part." She pressed a hand to her head. "Could I get something for a headache?"

"*Sí*, of course." Fernando hurried from the room.

Reed pulled Mona aside. "I don't think she'll be safe once the rustlers hear she lived. They won't want her identifying them in a lineup."

Mona looked to him, her brows furrowing. "What do you suggest we do?"

"I think she'll be okay here for the night, but then she should come back to the ranch where we can keep an eye on her. I'm sure the doctor will want her to lay low with the bruised ribs for a while. She won't be going back to work tomorrow."

"Okay."

After the nurse gave her something for her headache, Catalina drifted back to sleep.

Mona gave Fernando and Rosa strict instructions to stay with Catalina and bring her out to the ranch as soon as the doctor released her. They insisted Mona leave and take care of her ranch and Jesse.

Reed waited by the door until Mona was ready. At two in the morning, they left the hospital and headed back to the ranch, going straight out to the herd where Jesse sat on a camp stool, singing in his off-pitch, tone-deaf voice to over one thousand head of cattle. When they informed Jesse of the assault on Catalina he left immediately for Amarillo, leaving Reed and Mona in charge of the herd.

Even in the dim starlight, Reed could see that the grass was gone. The cattle would have to be released from this pasture by the next day or they'd be hungry.

He hoped his friend would come through with his

request soon. When they let the cattle out, he wanted to be prepared with a little surprise of his own.

CLOSE TO SUNUP, Mona climbed into bed and fell into a deep sleep. She'd have slept all the way through the day and into the next if not for the baby straining against her bladder. When she got up to relieve herself, the sound of a delivery truck bumping down the gravel driveway kept her from going back to bed. That and the thought of the dozen or so things that needed to be done on the ranch.

She crossed to her bedroom window in time to see Reed sign for a package. Finding it increasingly difficult, she bent to pull on a pair of jeans and tried to zip them. The zipper stopped halfway up, encountering her belly. The loose jeans Rosa had loaned her didn't even fit anymore. She left the zipper halfway down, pulled one of her father's cotton shirts on and rolled up the sleeves. Maternity clothes didn't do her much good on a ranch, the fabric was too flimsy to ride in and too easily stained. These would have to do.

Reed was out in the kitchen, slicing through packing tape to open the box.

"I don't remember ordering anything." Mona strode into the kitchen, brows raised.

"Might be because you didn't. Remember that phone call I mentioned last night before you got in the shower?"

She nodded.

"A buddy of mine quit the force and went into surveillance and private investigative work for people and animals. He sent twenty-five tracking devices and instructions on how we can locate them through a Web site." Reed held up small oval objects that looked like large ceramic pills. "Now all we have to do is get the cattle to swallow them."

"How does it work?"

"The device stays in their stomachs and, like the GPS devices on cars, can be tracked. We just have to log on to the computer and key in the tracking numbers." He gave her the once-over. "You up for feeding a few cows?"

"Sure am. The herd is due to be wormed in a couple weeks. We can move that operation up. Since we have them close to the corral and cattle chute, we should have no problem getting at least twenty-five to swallow the devices." For the first time in days, the sun was shining and she could almost see the end to the rustling problem. A smile spread across her face, hope bubbling up inside. She threw her arms around Reed's neck. "Thank you."

Reed stood stiff and unbending against her brief display of emotion.

When Mona drew away, her face heated. "Pardon me. I shouldn't have done that."

"Something you need to know." He placed all the devices back in the box, one at a time. "Once the cattle rustlers are caught, I'll be looking for a new job."

The happy butterflies in Mona's belly turned to stone and fell one by one, until her stomach felt empty, cold and leaden.

The man who'd stormed into her life, guns ablazin', would leave as soon as her troubles were over. She should have expected as much. Reed was destined for better things. Better than working a ranch. He had to be missing his work on the Chicago police force. Tracking down criminals and solving murders was much more interesting than trying to snag cattle rustlers on the Texas prairie.

Still, the ranch wouldn't be the same. The plains would be wider and emptier. Mona had to admit she liked riding with him and would miss him when he was gone.

Mona shook her head to halt her runaway train of thought before it derailed. "Is Jesse back from Amarillo?"

"Yes," Reed replied.

"Good. We can have the cattle tagged and out in the north pasture before the end of the day."

With a nod, Reed carried the box out the back door.

She watched through the window until he disappeared into the barn. A resolution was at hand. This solution would reveal who the rustlers were, once and for all. Then she could get back to all her other problems.

AFTER TREATING fifty head of cattle with worm medication, twenty-five of which had ingested the tracking devices, Reed, Jesse and Mona herded them to the north pasture where they could find fresh grass. The others they moved closer to the homestead. If the rustlers wanted cattle, they'd have to take the ones in the north pasture.

Reed hoped his plan worked. After a quick pass around the fence line, he insisted Mona go back to the house and rest. She looked tired and sore, pressing her hand to her belly on more than one occasion. When he returned to the house, he found her in the barn, feeding horses and mucking out stalls.

"Enough." He crossed the dirt floor and took the shovel away from her, setting it against the wall. "Go to the house. Now."

"The work has to be done." She attempted to reach around him for the tool.

He blocked her path. "I'll take care of it." Then he turned her around and gently pushed her toward the house. "Eat and get a shower. I'll come show you how to use the online locator in just a few minutes."

She pressed a hand to her lower back. "Okay. I guess I am tired." As she walked toward the barn door, she picked up a bucket and veered toward the grain bins.

Reed shook his head. The woman didn't know what it meant to quit. "Drop it, boss."

"What?" She looked around, a confused expression on her face. When he stared at the bucket in her hand, she blushed. "Oh. Okay." With a sheepish grin, she set the bucket on top of the feed bin. "Don't forget to give Topper half a can of sweet feed and a section of hay. He worked hard today. And Sassy still needs to be brushed."

Reed shot a narrow-eyed glare at her. "Go."

"Okay, okay." She scooted toward the door, muttering as she went, "Who's in charge around here anyway?"

Jesse led his horse into the barn, slipped the bridle off and snapped a lead onto his halter. "Miss Mona is one stubborn boss lady."

"Yes, indeed."

"But you won't find a better woman to work for in all of the panhandle." The young Latino tied his horse to a post and faced Reed. "She's fair and she cares about her people and the land."

"I noticed."

"She misses her father very much. With so much heartache, I'd hate to see her hurt more."

"Who would hurt her?" Reed scooped up a shovel of manure and tossed it into the wheelbarrow beside the stall.

Jesse lifted the saddle off his horse and slung it onto a saddletree. "The father of her child must have hurt her for her to keep him a secret. But I'm more concerned about you." He faced Reed. "Don't break her heart, Señor Bryson. She's a good woman."

After a couple more shovelsful of manure, he set the shovel to the side and lifted the handles of the wheelbarrow, heading toward the barn door. "I've no intention of breaking her heart. I'm only here to help bring in the rustlers. After that, I'll be on my way." He stepped out into the barnyard, away from the lecturing ranch hand, but not before he heard Jesse's parting comment.

"That's what I was afraid of."

Once the chores were complete, Reed entered the ranch house.

"I'll have something semi-edible on the table for you as soon as you've showered," Mona called out from the kitchen.

The scent of grilled onion drifted through the house, reminding Reed how hungry he was. He hurried through the shower and slipped into clean jeans and a black T-shirt. When he padded into the kitchen in bare feet, he wasn't prepared for the sight of Mona wearing a white dress. Tied just beneath her breasts, the soft fabric effectively hid the gentle swell of her belly. The flowing material draped down to just below her knees, displaying the tight lines of her calves and her bare feet. The stark white gave her dark skin a healthy glow.

With her hair piled high on her head in a loose ponytail, she looked young and fresh and…beautiful.

Reed's breath caught in his throat with a sense of longing so strong it made him take a step back, hitting his bare heel against the doorjamb. "Ouch!"

Mona turned, a smile on her face. "There you are.

Just in time." Her smile turned lopsided. "I'm not a cook, so you'll have to bear with me. I'm only good for breakfast. We're having *migas*." She scraped the contents of the skillet into a serving bowl and handed it to him. "If you'll set that on the table, I'll grab the orange juice."

While Reed lived in Chicago, he'd missed the Tex-Mex food he could only find in Texas. After seating Mona, Reed pulled up a chair at the small kitchen table and scooped fluffy yellow eggs, mixed with bell pepper, onion, tomatoes and tortilla chips onto his plate.

Mona tucked into the food, loading her plate as full as his. When she was halfway through the meal, she sat back and sighed. "I guess my eyes were much bigger than my stomach." She ran her hand over her belly. "I'll clean up. Why don't you bring up the Web site so we can check on the cattle."

"Let me help and we can get to it faster."

Mona washed and Reed dried the dishes. The entire process felt as intimate as the kiss he'd shared with Mona the previous night. With her by his side, he had to stop from reaching out and pulling her into his arms and stealing another kiss. He couldn't lead her on. She deserved a better man than him. One with a better understanding of fathering than he'd been brought up on.

Reed didn't linger. As soon as the dishes were dried and put away, he sat at the computer and followed the directions that came with the tracking devices. Soon he had the first cattle number loaded into the program and a satellite view came up with a red dot indicating where the animal was. Pretty much where they'd left them.

Mona stood behind him, bent over his shoulder staring at the screen.

He plugged in several more numbers, each indicating the cattle were still exactly where they were expected to be. "Think you can handle it?"

"No problem." She gave him a narrowed glance. "Why?"

"I want to go back to Leon's and see if I can find our man with the cut on his head."

She crossed her arms over her chest, her lips forming that stubborn line Reed recognized as her pigheaded look. "I'm going with you."

"What about the herd?" He stood, towering over her five-foot-three-inch frame. "You need to stay."

"We can leave Jesse here to monitor the GPS tracking system. If anything moves, he can call us."

"You don't need to be out so late. What about the baby?"

"I can do anything I did before I was pregnant." Her lips twisted a little. "Only a bit slower."

"Exactly. You should be resting. You put in a long day." He reached out, brushing his thumb beneath her eyes. "You have circles under your eyes."

"I'll be fine." Those whiskey-colored eyes stared back at him, knocking the breath out of his lungs. She squared her shoulders and looked toward the doorway. "Now, are we leaving or are you going to argue some more?"

"Are you sure you weren't a drill sergeant in your former life?" Reed returned to his room for socks and boots and met her outside by her pickup.

"I'll drive." She climbed into the driver's seat, giving him no option but to slide into the passenger side.

AT EIGHT-THIRTY on Saturday night, Leon's wasn't hopping yet. Only the locals had drifted in to gather around the bar. Reed seated Mona on an empty bar stool and stood behind her.

"How ya doin', Oscar?" Mona smiled at the bartender when he came to take their orders.

"Been a while since I've seen you in here." He chuckled. "Although I heard you were outside last night breakin' up a fight. Wished I'd seen that."

She shrugged. "Wasn't much to it. How's your wife? Did her surgery come out all right?"

"Sure did." He grinned. "She's a lot happier without those danged gallstones."

"I'll bet. Give her my regards, will you?"

"Sure will. Stop by sometime. I'm sure she'd love to see you." He wiped the counter in front of her. "What can I get you?"

"I'll have a straight ginger ale and we have a few questions to ask."

The bartender stared up at Reed and back to Mona as if he was sizing up the man. "Shoot."

Reed leaned over Mona's shoulder. "Were you working the night before last?"

"Yes," Oscar replied.

"Do you remember the five Hispanic men sitting in that corner?"

"Sure do. They're regulars on Friday and Saturday nights. They come in, sit in that exact corner and leave. They pretty much keep to themselves."

"Know any by name?"

"No."

The man sitting beside Mona turned to her. "If it's the guys I'm thinking of, they live in the trailer court down by the old silos."

Mona turned the full force of her smile on the man. "Thanks, Bobby. How's your little boy? Did he make the all-stars baseball league this year?"

Bobby's chest puffed out and he grinned. "Sure did. Kenny's the starting pitcher when they go to state."

"That's wonderful. Congratulations." Mona rested a hand on his arm. "You wouldn't happen to know exactly which trailer I could find them in, would you?"

The man shook his head. "No, but ask Les or Wayne. I've seen them talking on occasion."

"Les Newton and Wayne Fennel?" For a moment, Mona's smile slipped.

"Not much of a recommendation, is it? Those two

have been in trouble since they were kids back in high school."

"Yeah." She stared across the room as if looking for them. Then she sipped from her glass and set it on the counter. When Mona pulled a bill from her purse, Oscar waved her money away.

"It's on me. Come see us more often."

"I will. You take care and be sure to say hello to Dottie for me."

"Will do."

Mona got off the stool and looked up at Reed. "Ready?" Without waiting for a response, she led the way out of the bar, the pretty white dress a ray of sunshine in the dark and dirty establishment. The men present didn't wolf call or make rude comments, perhaps recognizing her for the lady she was.

Reed's mouth turned upward on the corners. The woman must know everyone in town and she had a way of getting them to open up. Not by flirting and coming on to them. Her genuine concern for their welfare and that of their families made the difference. Mona Grainger was the real thing.

He held the door for her as she climbed into the driver's seat of the ranch truck.

"This is as far as you go. Besides, you're not dressed to go chasing cattle rustlers."

"Who said we would chase them?" Her brows rose high on her forehead. "I just want to check on Rosa's cousin who lives in the neighborhood. What harm could come of that?" She barely waited for Reed to climb in before she shifted into reverse and left Leon's parking lot.

"I should have known Les and Wayne might have something to do with the rustling. They've always been trouble. I'm surprised the sheriff hasn't checked them out already."

"Who are they?"

"Les and Wayne were buddies back in high school. They set fires, tore up mailboxes and stole cars. They've been in and out of jail so many times, it wouldn't surprise me if they were involved." She shook her head. "Thing is, this cattle rustlin' takes someone with a few more brain cells than Les and Wayne put together. They might be involved, along with the guy you saw last night, but I'm betting someone else is supplying the cattle trucks and four-wheelers."

"If these guys are in the trailer court, you have no business being there."

"Like I said, I'm just going to visit Rosa's cousin. Maybe she can answer a few questions for us."

Reed agreed reluctantly because he wasn't the one driving. Had he been, he'd have turned the truck around and headed straight back to the Rancho Linda.

The trailer court was set back from the road, with the giant towers of the granary silos casting shadows over them. A few lights shone through tattered blinds on some of the trailers.

The creepy feeling that they were driving into a

trap crawled across Reed's skin. He found himself reaching for a gun at his belt. A gun that went along with wearing a law enforcement badge, both of which he didn't have on him tonight. "I have a bad feeling about this. We're not staying."

"I'm going to talk to Maria. You stay out here and be my lookout. Maybe you'll see something." She dropped down out of the truck and climbed the rickety steps to the first trailer in the lot, clutching the hem of her dress to keep the wind from blowing it upward. At least the little bit of a yard and the windows were clean. An older Hispanic woman with similar features to Rosa's opened the door and hurried Mona through. She stared around at the truck before closing the door behind her.

Reed waited in the shadows, letting his eyes adjust to the darkness. About the time he could make heads or tails of the dark shapes, a vehicle slowed on the highway and headlight beams turned into the trailer park.

Closing one eye to maintain his night vision, Reed ducked behind Maria's trailer and watched as a battered truck sped down the gravel road to the last trailer. Five men piled out.

One of the men banged his head on the roof of the truck and cursed, the dome light shining down on a nasty cut. The same five men from the bar the night before.

Reed was torn between waiting for Mona and

going after the men. The decision was taken from him when Maria's trailer door opened and Mona emerged.

Damn. She couldn't have had worse timing.

The men at the end of the road scattered like vermin.

"Go back inside," Reed called out in a loud whisper.

"No, I'm going with you."

"Like hell. Get inside or I'll throw you in the truck and take you straight home."

"You can't talk to me that way."

"The more you talk, the farther away they'll run. Now go inside and stay until I come back for you."

"There are five of them and one of you. How do you propose to stop all five?"

"Leave it to me and lock the door behind you."

Mona snorted, but thankfully walked back into the trailer. When the lock clicked, Reed took off at a run down the backside of the trailers in the direction the man with the cut had run.

A shadow disappeared between the first and second grain silos.

Reed raced after it, keeping close to the tree line until he reached the open area in front of the granary towers.

Unarmed, he'd be foolish to chase after a man into the country equivalent of a dark alley. He ran out into the open, headed for the corner of the silo, when a shot rang out, kicking up the gravel in front of him. Someone shouted in the dark, words Reed couldn't understand.

Dodging first to the right and then to the left, Reed

created an erratic zigzag pattern. Another shot rang out, the ground erupting behind him. Then he was at the corner of the tower. He slid around behind the structure into the shadows, straining to hear over the sound of his own breathing and the wail of the wind streaming between the silos.

He'd made a mistake. He shouldn't have left Mona at the trailer. What if the shooter circled back and took her hostage or shot her?

Feet shuffled in the gravel in front of the silos and another shot rang out, followed by a loud groan and a heavy thump.

From the direction of the trailer court, another shot popped off.

Reed hoped like hell Mona was lying on the floor of Maria's trailer, staying out of trouble.

A car engine revved, peeling out of the gravel parking lot onto the highway.

Careful so as not to create too big a target, Reed peered around the silo. Car taillights disappeared past the houses farther down the street.

On the gravel lay a man-size lump. It stirred and moaned.

Keeping low to the ground, Reed ran out to the figure sprawled in the shadows.

Flat on his back, with a gaping hole in his gut lay the man with the cut on his forehead. He reached out to Reed and grasped his arm. *"Traidor."*

"Qué?" Reed asked.

"Traid—" His eyes closed and his grip loosened on Reed's arm.

Reed felt for a pulse in his neck, but there wasn't one to find. The man was dead.

"He said traitor." Mona's voice startled Reed and he leaped to his feet. She stood with her hair being whipped around her face, her dress billowing around her body and a rifle in her hands.

"What the hell are you doing out here?"

"I heard gunshots. I tried to wait like you said, but I couldn't. You might have been hurt." She stared out at the road. "Lot of good it did, I missed the shooter. Heck, I didn't even hit the car."

"You and the baby could have been killed."

"I stayed in the shadows of the trailer as much as possible. I wouldn't put my baby at risk."

He grabbed her arm. As he turned her toward Maria's trailer, sirens wailed across the small town.

"Great." Before he could get Mona away from the dead man, a sheriff's SUV swung off the road and skidded to a stop in the gravel. Toby Braxton jumped from the car and pointed his pistol at Reed and Mona. "Drop the gun!"

Chapter Nine

"Well, well, well. If it isn't the female rancher and her hired gun." Parker Lee circled Mona and Reed sitting in the sheriff's office, both cuffed. "Interesting that Miss Grainger was the one caught holding the smoking gun."

Mona bit hard on her lip to keep from spewing the scathing remarks she wanted so badly to say. Now wasn't the time to tell Parker Lee exactly what she thought of him. The way it looked out at the granary made her appear like the shooter.

"She didn't shoot the man I found." Reed stood, his brows drawn in a deep frown. "Someone in a car did. She was shooting at the man who did the killing."

"Sit down, Bryson." Sheriff Lee shoved against Reed's chest.

Reed stood solid, glaring at the sheriff, in a staring standoff. When Parker Lee looked away, Reed took his seat.

Mona's heart swelled at Reed's defense. She had

to admit, on the surface, the evidence was damning. One man dead and she was the one holding a rifle that had been fired recently.

Lee leaned into Reed. "No one reported a car, and you were the only other person there. Does that mean you shot the man?"

Reed glared back at the man. "There *was* a car and if you do a ballistics report on the bullet, you'll see that Mona didn't kill that man. You're wasting your time arresting us."

"You can go, Bryson, but Miss Grainger has to stay until the judge sets bail. Not that she can post that bail. Can you, Mona?" He touched a finger to her chin and lifted her face. "Told you that ranch was too much for you to handle."

The touch of the sheriff's finger on her chin made her skin crawl and her rage burn. "Up yours, Parker. Rancho Linda has been in my family for a long time. It's staying in my family."

"Kinda hard to run a ranch from the inside of a jail cell."

Reed stood. "Look, you can't put her in jail, she's pr—"

"Leave it, Reed." She stared hard at him, willing him to understand and not say anything about her pregnancy. Not now. The only people who knew were Fernando, Rosa, Catalina and now Reed. She'd never bothered to tell Jesse or Dusty, and she sure as hell didn't want Parker Lee to know anything about the child growing in her belly. The man was vindictive and would use the knowledge against her.

Two portly, gray-haired men stepped into the sheriff's office. One wore a short-sleeved pullover and khaki slacks, the other a wrinkled oxford cotton shirt rolled at the sleeves and gray suit slacks.

The man in the oxford shirt went straight to Mona and engulfed her in a hug. "Mona, Maria called as soon as she saw what was happening."

"Oh, Mr. Wallendorf, I'm so glad you're here." Greg Wallendorf had gone to high school with her father, and had been one of his fishing and poker buddies for the past thirty years. He was also an attorney. She quickly gave him the lowdown.

"That's pretty much what Maria said. I brought the judge with me to set bail." He leaned into Mona and whispered, "You were in luck. It was our poker night."

Mona didn't feel so lucky, but given the circumstances, she counted her blessings.

"Judge Stevenson, glad you could make it." Sheriff Lee held out his hand to the man, looking less than glad the judge was there. "Miss Grainger is the prime suspect in the murder of an illegal alien."

"What kind of hooey is this?" Judge Stevenson had stood by while Mona gave her attorney the details. Now he moved around Sheriff Lee to stand in front of Mona.

Surely this man who'd been another of her father's

friends for years would see reason. Hope sprang in her chest. "Sir, I didn't shoot the man."

Parker Lee pulled Toby Braxton in from the outer offices. "Tell him what you saw."

"I got a call from dispatch that gunshots were fired near the old granary. When I got there, I found her—" he poked his finger in Mona's face "—holding a rifle standing over the dead man. She was the only one around holding a gun, the gun had been fired and the man was dead. I arrested her on suspicion of murder and read her the Miranda rights."

Judge Stevenson turned to Mona. "I'm sorry. Based on the initial evidence, they had a right to arrest you."

Sheriff Lee stepped forward. "We request that you don't set bail. She could be dangerous to the community, possibly go out and shoot someone else."

The judge snorted. "I have no doubt Miss Grainger didn't shoot the man, but given the evidence, I'll have to set bail at one hundred thousand dollars. Contact my secretary tomorrow to schedule the court hearing. Now, if you'll excuse me, I'm late getting home." With that, the judge left.

Bile rose in Mona's throat. One hundred thousand dollars? She couldn't come up with fifty thousand to save her ranch, how the heck was she going to post bail? Even though she knew she'd be cleared of the charges, how would the banks look at her credit application when she'd been arrested on suspicion of murder?

Parker's smug smile grated on Mona's last nerve. "Let Bryson go, Miss Grainger stays until bail is posted."

Toby unlocked Reed's cuffs, jerking them off his hand with more force than necessary. "Get out of here."

"Not until I've talked with Miss Grainger."

"Sorry, gotta lock her up." Toby's brows rose in challenge. "Unless you got one hundred thousand to bail her pretty little butt out."

Reed stared across at Mona, the muscle in his jaw twitching. "I'll get the money."

"Uncle Arty is the only family I have left." She'd sworn she'd never talk to her uncle, least of all beg him for money, after the way he'd treated her mother and father all these years. Unfortunately, Uncle Arty might be her last hope.

"I'll get the money." Reed turned to Parker Lee. "You hurt her and…"

"And what?" Parker sneered. "She's a murderer. I might have to defend myself against her."

Toby tugged her arm, propelling her to the back of the sheriff's office where the jail cells were located.

Greg Wallendorf stared across the linoleum-tile floor of the sheriff's office, first at Toby and then at the sheriff. "Either one of you hurt her, and I'll have you both locked up so fast, you won't know what hit you."

The last Mona saw was the killing look Reed gave Sheriff Lee before he stormed out behind her attorney.

The metal clank of the bars being closed and

locked behind her brought home the depth of her troubles. Mona sank to the cot, her knees no longer capable of holding her up.

Now what?

"MR. BRYSON." What did he call a man who wasn't his real father? "It's me, Reed." Coming to his stepfather in the middle of the night wasn't something he relished, but he didn't have many choices.

After the attorney dropped him off at Mona's truck, Reed had tried to find a bail bondsman, but the closest one was in Amarillo. The thought of spending an hour on the road to and from was more than Reed could stomach. Every minute Mona was in that jail was a minute too long. He knew how much she hated going to Arty for the money, thus his plea to the only other man he knew who might have that kind of money lying around.

"Reed?" Will Bryson opened the door, his graying hair standing on end as though he'd just risen from his bed. "What's the matter?"

"I need help."

"Come in." He motioned toward the living room. "Your mother's still sleeping. I'd like to keep it that way, if we can."

"Good, I'd rather not worry her." Reed took a deep breath and launched in. "My boss, Mona Grainger, has been arrested and I need one hundred thousand dollars to bail her out of jail tonight."

In the process of taking a seat in the leather armchair, Will Bryson sat down hard, his eyes wide. "What did you say?"

Reed's gut twisted. "Miss Grainger's been arrested and I need money to bail her out. I'll pay you back as soon as she's cleared of the charges."

"On what grounds was she arrested?"

Here it went. Reed stared across at his stepfather. "Suspicion of murder."

The man's face paled. "Did she kill someone?"

"No." Reed stood. Coming here was a mistake.

"How do you know she didn't? How do you know that if you bail her out she won't kill again?"

"Because I know. Mona Grainger is not a killer."

"Did you see who killed the man?"

"No." Reed pushed a hand through his hair and dropped it to his side. "Never mind. Thanks for letting me in. I can show myself out."

"Reed." His stepfather followed him to the door and laid a hand on his arm when he reached for the knob. "I'm just trying to understand."

"That's just it. Sometimes you can't understand everything, you have to go with your heart. You have to care enough about someone to believe in them. Even in uncertain circumstances." Reed shook off William Bryson's hand and left, closing the door behind him. As far as he was concerned, his stepfather had failed him yet again.

Which didn't solve his immediate problem.

Reed turned his truck toward the nearest convenience store, where he borrowed a phone book and looked up Arty Grainger's number. With his last bit of change, he dialed from the pay phone on the corner.

SOMETIME AFTER ONE in the morning, Mona must have fallen asleep on the dirty bare mattress. Even before she heard the metal jingle of keys, thunder woke her, banging loud enough to rattle the light fixtures in her cell.

"You can go." Parker Lee held the bars open, a sneer curling the edge of his lip all the way up to the flare of his nose. "Just don't leave town. If I had my way, I'd keep you locked up until your trial."

Mona ignored him, too tired to care enough to form an appropriate response.

Reed stood on the other side of the room, his lips pressed together in a tight line.

Even during the darkest hours of her despair, she'd known he'd somehow come through for her.

Tears welled in her eyes and clogged her throat. She collected her belongings from the deputy and walked outside into a blasting wind, hanging on tightly to her control and the hem of her dress.

When she normally would have taken the driver's seat, she knew better and headed for the passenger side.

Reed was there before her to open the door and hand her up into the seat.

On the verge of bawling her eyes out, she pushed

her hair out of her eyes and stared straight ahead, focusing on the single streetlight illuminating the sheriff's office parking lot. *Let me hold on until we get away from Parker Lee.*

The wind blew against the side of the pickup in blustering gusts. Reed's fingers turned white with the amount of strength he used to keep the vehicle on the road.

Half a mile out of town, Mona said, "Pull over."

One look at her and Reed slowed to a halt on the wide shoulder.

Mona jumped down from the truck and bent double, emptying the meager contents of her stomach on the Texas prairie grass, pushed over by the wind.

A hand gathered her hair up behind her and out of the way. Another reached around her shoulders and held her until she was completely empty.

Lightning illuminated the sky, thunder booming with every strike. "We can't stay out here for long," Reed shouted over the roar of the wind. "This is tornado weather."

When she could stand straight again, she looked up into Reed's eyes, tears streaming from her own. "Thank you for coming."

"I wouldn't let you stay there." He smiled, and dabbed at her eyes with a crisp white handkerchief. "Come on. Let's get you out of this storm."

She let him help her back into the truck, where she laid her head back against the seat and drifted in and out of sleep, the rocking motion of the truck being buffeted by the wind more comforting than frightening.

When they arrived in front of the house, Jesse ran out onto the porch, flinching when a flash of lightning lit the darkened sky. "The cattle are moving!"

All remnants of sleep vanished with a spurt of adrenaline and Mona dropped to the ground, running. She ducked into her bedroom and emerged minutes later wearing jeans and a soft blue, cotton shirt, tugging socks and boots onto her bare feet.

Reed was first to the computer. A blinking dot moved across the screen in a steady motion. With a few quick clicks, Reed brought up the next cow's number and it too was moving in the same direction, northeast toward the Palo Duro Canyon and, from what he could tell, on the outside border of Rancho Linda. Rough country for a vehicle.

A brilliant flash lit the window, followed closely by an ear-splitting bang, and the lights blinked and then extinguished inside the house. The computer screen faded to black in a few short seconds.

"Damn." She fumbled inside a desk drawer for matches, lighting the scented candle on the shelf above the dark monitor. "How can we follow them without the computer?"

The soft candle glow encased Reed in warm light. "Jesse and I will ride out."

"The terrain out there is too rough for trucks and we only have one four-wheeler. There's a gravel road near the canyon, but to get to it would take an hour by road. It'll only take thirty minutes by horseback," Mona said. "Let's go."

With one step to the side, Reed blocked her exit. "You're not going anywhere. You've already been through enough."

Mona bristled. "I'm the boss, in case you haven't heard."

Reed glanced over his shoulder at Jesse, hovering in the doorway. "Saddle up our horses and grab a rifle."

Once Jesse left the house, Reed reached out, gripped Mona's arms and shook her gently. "Be reasonable."

"I have to go, Reed. That's my livelihood out there. They're threatening my property. I'm being as reasonable as I possibly can."

"And you'd risk your baby?"

For a moment Mona couldn't say anything, she'd never considered losing the child. She'd had the crazy notion she could ride, fence and ranch up to the day she delivered. An image of her at nine months along trying to climb onto a horse found its way into her mind and the ridiculousness made her mouth quirk. But the thought of someone making off with her herd made her hackles rise. "Okay, I'll take it easy, but I'm going. I'll even let you carry the gun. I haven't had much luck with the law and guns lately."

"I'd rather you stayed here."

She wiggled, trying to get free. "You're just like the rest of the men who want to run my life for me."

He refused to let her go, increasing the pressure on her arms until her chest bumped up against his. "No. I think you—of all the women and men I've ever known—you can handle ranching better than any of them."

"You're just saying that to get me to stay." She squirmed, the movement only aggravating her awareness of him standing so close their thighs touched. Her body was on fire, not with anger but desire. And that scared her more than a pit full of diamondback rattlesnakes.

"No, I'm not just saying that to get you to stay, but if it helps, good. You have to start thinking about yourself and your baby." He wrapped her in his arms.

Mona told herself she couldn't breathe because of how tightly he held her, but the truth was, her breathing was short and shallow because of her reaction to his body against hers. He made her body burn. "Why do you care?"

"Hell if I know. I just do." Then he was kissing her, hard and long. Before she could begin to think, his hands were combing through her hair, bringing her lips impossibly closer.

Mona's lips parted and Reed's tongue delved in, past her teeth to tangle with and taste her tongue.

When his lips tore free, she stared up at him, her eyes wide, her breathing ragged. What had he just done to her? He'd made her completely forget for a moment anything to do with Rancho Linda and her heritage. For a moment all she wanted was for him to kiss her again.

The baby kicked against her belly hard enough to make her jerk.

Reed jumped back, moving her to arm's length. "Was that the baby?" A look of wonder spread across his rugged face.

"Yes." Grasping at her chance to regain control of her emotions and the situation, she backed away from Reed. "He wasn't too happy about being squashed between the two of us. And he's just as determined to protect his heritage as I am. So if it's all the same to you, I'd like to get moving." *Before I go back for seconds on that kiss.* Her mind and lips numb, she stumbled for the door.

He grabbed her arm, his fingers firm but gentle. "You're staying."

"I'm not, so let's quit wasting time and saddle up before they get away with the herd." She didn't give him a chance to argue. Instead, she shook off his hold and left the house, striding toward the barn in long desperate steps, her thoughts as tumultuous as the stormy sky.

Jesse must have known she'd win the battle, because he had her horse saddled and waiting next to two others. They stamped in the dust, eyes flaring with each strike of lightning and rumble of thunder. Chewy whimpered beside Jesse, staring up at him, awaiting his command and determined not to be left behind.

Wind blasted across the prairie like a freight train, pushing the grass flat and forcing the riders and horses to lean against it to remain upright.

Crazy to leave the relative safety of the house in such wicked weather, Mona gritted her teeth and moved on, tired beyond words, but determined to save what was left of her cattle.

Halfway out to the north pasture, Mona sent Jesse and Chewy to the central pasture to check the herd there. She kept Reed with her, suspecting the cattle in the north were the only ones targeted in this run.

In silence, they rode over hills and down into rugged gullies to get to the far northeast corner of her property. Uncle Arty's ranch bordered on the northeast and the Palo Duro Canyon lay due north of Rancho Linda.

On the border of her uncle's property, close to a gravel county road, they found the fence down and no cattle in sight.

Damn, had they already loaded them and taken off? A lead weight hit the pit of Mona's stomach. She couldn't lose again. She'd be ruined.

Reed shone his light on the ground where the dry earth had been sifted by hundreds of hoofprints. The wind lifted the dust and sandblasted Mona's skin. "They can't have gone far and they didn't have enough time to load them yet." Reed stared out over the prairie.

Mona nudged her horse forward. "Come on, we have to find them."

The cowboy jabbed his heels into his horse's flanks, causing the animal to rear up in front of Mona. "No." In the sporadic light from the flashes of lightning, he looked like the legendary Zorro ready to ride for justice.

An unexpected thrill raced through Mona's chest. One she quickly tamped down. "Cute." Her shouted sarcasm was lost in the raging wind. "But it's not stopping me."

"You can't charge into a pack of rustlers. Most likely, they're armed and prepared to shoot."

"I can't let them take my cattle." She dragged in a breath of dusty air and let it out. "I'll hang back. But we have to see who's doing this in order for us to catch them." When he didn't move, she planted her fist on her hip and ground out, "I didn't hire you to stop me. I hired you to help me."

For a moment more he hesitated, then he jerked his reins, aiming his horse in the direction the hoofprints led.

When Mona moved forward she could swear she heard Reed mutter something along the lines of "Lord save me from stubborn women." She could have been mistaken, but she didn't think so.

A smile tilted the corner of her lips as she set her horse into a gallop. "Women? Or woman?" she tossed over her shoulder, catching a glimpse of his stern face in a flash from the heavens above.

His lips set in a firm line, Reed caught up with her

and moved ahead, providing a barrier between her and any danger they might encounter.

As they neared a rise in the terrain, Reed reined in and slipped from his saddle. "We walk from here." He reached up and helped Mona from her horse, setting her gently on her feet. He stared up at the sky. "Won't be long before the sky opens up. I wouldn't be surprised if there's some hail and maybe a tornado out of that front moving our way." A brilliant flash lit the sky and thunder cracked nearby.

Both Reed and Mona ducked instinctively. The horses reared, dragging them away from the top of the hill, apparently having more sense than the humans for being out on a night like this.

Reed walked ahead up the small hill, Mona tagging along behind. When they topped the ridge, they peered down into the entrance to a canyon, probably a branch of the Palo Duro.

"There they are." Reed grabbed her wrist and pulled her close to the ground, pointing to the shadows at the base of a cliff.

She had to wait for another flash of lightning before she could see what he pointed at.

A ring of portable corral panels had been erected and her cattle were penned inside, their frightened bellows rising into the night air.

Rage ripped through Mona and she fought hard to control her first inclination to charge down there and tear down the panels. No, she had to keep her cool.

Reed's head turned right then left, his brows furrowing. "Where are the rustlers?"

For the first time, Mona noticed the cattle were there but the rustlers weren't. A chill swept down her spine that had nothing to do with the cool wind slashing her hair against her face.

Her eyes wide, she stared across at Reed. "You don't suppose they went back to get the other herd in the central pasture?" Jesse could be riding into a trap, while she and Reed sat there staring at a captured herd. "Come on." Mona ran toward her horse, grabbed the reins and attempted to stick her foot in the stirrup. It took her two tries with her belly getting in the way. When she finally had her foot anchored, she prepared to swing her leg over the top. Strong hands lifted her from behind and set her in her seat.

Reed swung up onto his horse in one fluid motion.

As Mona spun her mount back in the direction of the central pasture, the sound of multiple small engines alerted her to the fact they were no longer the only humans there. Half a dozen small headlights raced across the empty prairie, bumping over the dried clumps of grass and sage, headed directly toward them.

At first, Mona thought to ride right past them and back in the direction of the house. She pulled the revolver her father had given to her out of the holster strapped to her thigh and aimed at one of the lights. Before she could pull the trigger, the sharp crack of gunfire ripped through the air. Her horse reared, the revolver flew from her hands and it was all she could do to hold on and not be dumped in the midst of a pack of rustlers. Mona yanked the reins, turning the horse in the direction of the canyon and dug her heels into its flanks. As she raced across the prairie, the first fat drops of rain splashed into her eyes.

Chapter Ten

Reed raced after Mona, placing his body and horse directly behind her, hoping the bullets flying toward them wouldn't knock the woman from her horse. He prayed the storm would hold off until they could find a safe place to hide. His prayers went unanswered. Rain pelted him as his horse picked up speed, galloping across the open prairie toward the maze of canyon walls.

They skirted the pen of cattle, headed into the twisting, turning paths that led into the gorge.

His horse stumbled on the rocky ground, terrain four-wheelers could negotiate just as easily, if not better. A horse could break a leg or rear up and dump its rider on the ground, injuring both Mona and her baby or leaving them vulnerable to the thieves.

His pulse hammering against his temples, Reed raced at a breakneck speed following the brave woman ahead of him.

When she made a sharp turn into what looked like

a dead-end ravine, he almost shouted out his frustration. They'd be trapped. And then what? Would the thieves kill them to keep their identity a secret? Or post an armed guard until they were finished loading the cattle?

Reed wasn't taking any chances on the former. The latter option he could handle. A herd of cattle wasn't worth Mona's life, or the baby's. They should have stayed back at the ranch and waited until the rustlers had taken the cattle, then called the state police to stop the truck. Surely the electricity would have come back on within minutes. If not, they could have gone into town and used the computers at the library the next day to track the cattle.

His hindsight wasn't doing him any good at this point, when all his focus was needed to negotiate the darkened trail only lit with increasing intensity by the storm swirling overhead.

The trail narrowed into a rocky ravine fit only for agile animals, not four-wheelers. When he emerged at the top, Reed looked back. In the meager lightening flashes, he could see three foolish bikers careening up the pass after them. One of them flipped, the four-wheeler tumbling over the top of him and back down the steep draw, just missing the last one coming up.

"Come on!" Mona called out. She raced her horse across a flat plateau that led to another ravine snaking upward to the top of the canyon. At the base of the ravine, she dropped out of her saddle and slapped the horse's behind, sending him up the trail riderless. Then she ran toward the bluffs, disappearing into the shadows.

Reed swung out of his saddle, grabbed the rifle from the scabbard and slapped his horse's flanks. Startled by the slap, the gelding bucked forward and followed the mare up the ravine.

As Reed dived for the shadows, the two four-wheelers leaped over the edge and onto the plateau.

One rider paused, racing his engine, then he turned in a slow circle panning the flat area, searching for his quarry.

When the light turned in Reed's direction, he hugged the ground, lying across his rifle, closing his eyes to avoid any glare off metal or pupils.

The engines roared like raging lions and gunshots blasted into the night, mixing with the sound of thunder. He resisted the urge to cover his ears, knowing any movement could give him away. Rain dripped across Reed's forehead and down the back of his neck, but he remained motionless.

The noise went on for only half a minute, then everything stopped. Silence reigned except for the shouts from the rustlers gathering the cattle far below and the booming thunder echoing against the cliffs.

What were they waiting on? If Reed thought he could take both of them out without risking Mona, he would attack. But if he shot at them, they'd shoot back. With Mona somewhere behind him, he couldn't risk a bullet finding her in the shadows.

Rocks trickled down the upper ravine and the sound of a horse's whinny high above the plateau caught the riders' attention.

Engines roared to life and the four-wheelers shot up the steep, rocky embankment. With the rain increasing in force, the ravine turned into a stream, slowing their progress.

Reed lay still for several seconds longer, before low-crawling through the mud and deeper into the shadows.

"Mona?" he called out softly.

"Here."

He moved toward the sound of her voice, feeling his way along the base of the cliff until he bumped into something soft.

Her small hand shot out and captured his arm, dropping down to clasp his hand.

"Are you all right?" He touched her face in the darkness, only a silhouette of her image visible and the whites of her eyes glowing pale gray in the inky blackness of the cliff's shadow. A flash of lightning illuminated her face, highlighting wide, brown eyes and tan skin.

"I'm fine. I was more concerned about you." She leaned her cheek into his palm briefly and then straightened. "They'll be back in a minute when they figure out we ditched the horses."

Reed glanced around at the impenetrable face of

the cliffs. The wind blew so hard, he bent double under the pressure. "If this storm gets any worse, they won't be worried so much about us." A quick glance at the clouds lit by lightning confirmed his worse fears. The green tinge and swirling tails dipping toward the ground meant something to be feared more than rustlers. A tornado.

Mona tugged at his hand. "Come on. I know a place to hide."

MONA INCHED ALONG the base of the cliff. Brief flashes of lightning lit her path to the cliff caves she had explored with Catalina and Jesse when they were younger. If she was where she thought she was, there were caves close by.

Rocks, small tree limbs and other debris flew through the air, tossed about by the raging storm. Just as she was beginning to think she had the wrong place, the first pellets of hail rained down on her shoulders and a black gaping maw opened up in the side of the bluff.

The cave!

Mona ducked into the entrance as the sky broke open. Rain fell in sheets, interspersed with pea-size hail, growing as large as marbles.

Reed crowded in behind her, the overhang of the cliff sheltering them from the worst the storm had to offer.

When the wind drove the rain and hail into the cave's opening, Reed wrapped his arms around her and hauled her deeper into the dark interior.

Her skin and clothes soaked through by the rain, Mona shivered. "Think there are any animals in here with us?" The words came out between the chattering of her teeth.

"If there were, we'd have heard them by now." He stood still in the darkness, his hands resting lightly on her arms.

Surrounded by inky blackness, Mona thanked her Texas stars she was with Reed. His strength made her feel as if the storm and the rustlers couldn't touch her here. Then he dropped his hold on her arms and the cold enveloped her like an icy shroud.

With every flash of lightning, Reed moved a little farther away, searching the cave's interior. "Looks safe enough for now. Maybe the storm will thwart the rustlers and they'll give up and go home."

"Preferably, without my cattle."

For a few short minutes, neither spoke until Reed broke the silence. "Why didn't you want me to tell the sheriff you were pregnant?"

Mona sucked in a breath and let it out. After her run-in with the sheriff, she knew Reed would ask her sooner or later about her reluctance to spill the news. But why here? Why now, when so much had happened? "I have my reasons."

"If you go to town much longer, someone is bound to notice."

"Then I won't go to town."

"What about when you deliver?"

"That'll be in Amarillo."

"If you make it there in time." His fingers found her in the dark, curling around her arms. "What if you need to call 911?"

"I won't." She'd rather cross her legs for a hundred miles than allow the news of her child's birth be announced over the local dispatcher's radio. Her life and that of her baby could be at risk if a certain person were to find out the owner of Rancho Linda was expecting.

"What about when you bring the baby home?" Reed asked. "How will you explain it then?"

"I'll say I adopted it." She turned away, knowing her secret would get out, but refusing to cross that bridge until she had to.

A chill coursed across her skin. Now that she could slow down and get a grasp on the situation, the shock of being shot at sank in along with the worry of keeping her baby's lineage a secret. Her shivers intensified to body-racking tremors. "I c-c-can't s-stop sh-shaking."

Reed folded her into his arms and held her close, rubbing his hands up and down her back. "You're soaked to the skin." He tugged her chambray shirt up high enough that he could place his warm hands against the cold skin of her lower back. Heat radiated from that point outward.

Giving in to the temptation, Mona laid her head against his chest, finding his wet clothing warmed by the hot-blooded skin beneath. He smelled of prairie, rain and leather. Her breath caught in her throat and held as wild and dangerous thoughts of unbuttoning his shirt and running her hands over his chest raced through her consciousness.

From chillingly cold to steaming hot in the space of minutes, Mona snuggled closer. Gone from her mind were the worries of the rustlers finding her, the cattle being lost and the storm churning outside. Inside the cozy little cave, a storm of much greater intensity raged.

All her resolutions to steer clear of men, her self-induced celibacy, slid from rational thought into the moisture drenching her inside, preparing her for what she really wanted. To be with this man in the most intimate way, here in the dark, in a cave, in a storm.

Reed's hands skimmed over her back and downward to the curve of her hips, tugging her closer.

A moan rose up between them. Mona wasn't sure whether it was her or him, nor did she care. Thick denim stood in the way of feeding her desire. She pressed nearer to him, wrapping one leg around the back of his so that she could rub her aching need against his thickly muscled thigh.

Rough fingers laced through her hair, dragging her face closer, then he claimed her lips in a slanting kiss, grinding over her teeth and plundering deep into her mouth.

She gave as good as she got, her arms circling his

neck, her hands cupping the back of his head. Wanting more than a kiss, more than pressing soaked, fully clothed bodies against each other, she craved skin-to-skin contact. Her hands found their way between them, jerking at the buttons of his shirt until they loosened or popped free of the thread holding them. When she reached the waistline of his jeans, she didn't stop there. The hard metal button proved difficult, but she was up to the challenge and soon had it loose, reaching for the zipper.

His hand closed over hers. "Are you sure this is what you want? Aren't you afraid?" The flash of lightning blasted the dark interior of the cave, showing the sincerity in his face. The lines around his mouth also confirmed the amount of restraint he exerted to let her stop at this point.

"I've never been more sure of anything in my life." *Or more afraid.* Her hand dragged the zipper downward. Rain, hail and thunder beat against the cliffs, echoing the thrumming of blood through her veins. She couldn't go back now.

When he sprang free into her hands, she rejoiced that he was a man who preferred to ride commando, nothing but jeans.

His hands had risen during her desperate efforts to strip him of his clothing, working the buttons and zipper of her own. When it came to the part where Reed shoved her shirt down over her shoulders, Mona gulped, thanking the heavens for the cloudy night and the dark interior of the cave. With a protruding belly and overly large breasts, she wasn't in the best shape.

He dragged her pants down her legs, helping her to step out of her boots and then the jeans one leg at a time, careful not to unbalance her.

Finally she stood naked in the darkness, cool air caressing her feverish body.

Reed's hands trailed from her ankles upward, massaging her calves and thighs, his fingers working magic, steadily climbing upward until they found the sweet spot.

Mona cried out, leaning into his palm, touching her forehead to his chest, her breaths coming in labored puffs.

His fingers stopped their slow torture. "Am I hurting you?"

"Yes, in the best possible way." She laid her hand over his. "Don't stop now. That would hurt even more."

Her hands explored his shoulders and chest, tweaking the hard buttons of his nipples. She wished she had more light so that she could see the muscles rippling beneath her. Instead, she explored by touch alone, a heady sensation, cloaked in mystery and unabashed wonder.

Wind howled outside their haven and rain pounded on the rocks, creating a waterfall at the cave entrance. The effect was a constant roaring to match the blood pounding in her ears, blocking out the question threatening to break through her haze of desire. What was she thinking?

Reed bent and took the tip of her breast into his mouth, sucking gently then rolling the beaded tip with his tongue.

Mona's head lolled back, her hair brushing against her bottom. The answer to her question reverberated against the walls of the cave in a long, low moan originating from deep in her throat.

She didn't care what she was thinking as long as Reed kept doing what he was doing to make her forget everything else.

He walked her backward until her backside bumped against smooth, cool stone. There he hiked her up, careful not to jostle her belly, wrapping her legs around his waist.

With his hands on her hips, he guided her down over him, filling her slowly. "Tell me if it hurts. We'll stop."

"Please, don't stop." She eased lower, wary of the baby inside, but unwilling to give up the sensations filling her, stretching her to accommodate his length and girth.

Only five and a half months since she'd had sex, and then with a man who'd later shown his true colors, she was tight and feeling it. Loneliness had driven her into the arms of the wrong man before. Loneliness wasn't what drove her into Reed's arms now. Hot, raging passion compelled her to fall into the hired hand's arms. All she wanted was to slake her desires and be done with him. After all, she was a woman with certain needs demanding to be met by this man.

This time when she made love, she had nothing to lose…but her heart.

Chapter Eleven

Reed lay awake with Mona cradled in his arms for at least an hour after they collapsed on the pile of their clothing. She'd fallen asleep, exhausted from the chase and their lovemaking.

His hand found its way to the swell of her belly, gently stroking the soft skin. A tiny heel or elbow jabbed against his hand and he smiled in the darkness.

Was it a boy? Who would teach him how to play football, dribble a basketball or ride a horse? Who would instruct him in the merits of hard work and honesty? Who would teach him how to love and cherish a woman? A woman like Mona.

Reed's hand rose to her hair, pushing it back from her face. He cupped her cheek, reveling at the silken smoothness of her skin.

Based on her response to his questions the night before, he'd guessed the father of this baby was none other than Sheriff Parker Lee. Why else would Mona be so angry with the man and determined to keep the secret from all the local law enforcement?

No matter who the father was, the child was Mona's and she'd do anything to protect it. But would that be enough? Parker Lee had a ruthless streak. From the five months Reed had known him, he'd seen him use information to bring others down or hurt their careers. If Lee found out he was the father, would he try to take the child away from Mona?

Reed hugged Mona closer. She was a strong and determined woman, but would she be strong enough to hold up under the kind of pressure Parker Lee could exert?

He must have dozed. When he woke, he found himself lying across the ground naked, his clothing the only cushion between him and the hard stone.

The cool night air made him sit up and take stock. The woman who'd fallen asleep in his arms after thoroughly satisfying lovemaking was gone.

His pulse leaped and he scrambled to his feet, grabbing for his jeans. "Mona?"

"I'm here." Her voice sounded from the entrance to the cave. A faint glow illuminated her silhouette. "The storm is over and the sun will rise soon."

From the sound of her voice, that wasn't all that was over. Was she already regretting what they'd done?

Reed had mixed feelings. On the one hand, he'd thought to solve Mona's problems and disappear, refusing to become a permanent fixture in the Texas panhandle ever again. But riding beside her and running a ranch reminded him that he'd missed it. The hard work, constant upkeep and getting your hands dirty made a man remember why he was strong.

He dressed and joined Mona at the cave's entrance.

She stood with her back to him, staring out at the canyon. "I don't see any signs of our four-wheelin' friends. Suppose they've gone?"

"I'd bet they're long gone. Let's go see if they made off with the cattle." Reed gripped Mona's hand and led the way down the narrow path. Moonlight guided their efforts with the pale promise of morning easing upward in the east. All storm clouds had cleared.

Mona tried to pull her hand loose, but Reed refused to let go, insisting on helping her over the boulders and loose gravel. When they reached the canyon floor, they moved along the base of the cliff, careful to stay out of plain sight in case the rustlers were hiding amongst the boulders.

When they reached the area where the corralled cattle had been, nothing but a churned-up muddy quagmire remained. Tire tracks from what looked like an eighteen-wheeler left deep ruts in the ground, deeper than normal, as though the rig had bogged down, possibly having gotten stuck.

The more Reed walked around the churned-up area, the more mud caked his boots, weighing him down. He glanced across at Mona as she struggled to take one step at a time.

"I don't see the cattle, but I can't imagine getting

out of here with a fully loaded truck. Maybe there's hope?" She gave him half a smile. "Come on, we need to get back to the ranch house and it's a good five miles from here." Not much on horseback, but a long walk on foot.

As Reed crossed over the cut fence, he noticed a distant rider on horseback, leading another horse and headed their way. He moved in front of Mona in case the rider wasn't friendly. The closer the lone horseman came, the tenser Reed became until he could make out the man's features.

"It's Fernando. Thank God." Mona moved around Reed and closed the distance between her and the ranch foreman. "Fernando, I'm so glad you're here. Everything all right at the hospital?"

"Catalina is anxious to get home. The doctor will release her later today. I just couldn't stay not knowing what was going on at the Rancho Linda."

Mona shook here head. "I'm glad you came." She filled him in on the missing herd. Then she glanced at him, concern pulling her brows together. "Jesse wasn't at the ranch when you got in?"

"No, *señorita*." Fernando shook his head. "But all three horses were at the barn, still saddled."

Reed assisted Mona up into the saddle of the spare horse. "Come on. We have to find him." His gut told him to hurry.

Mona moved her foot out of the stirrup for Reed to place his booted foot in. He swung up behind

Mona and wrapped his arms around her waist. "Let's go."

Nudging her horse into a gallop, Mona headed for the central pasture where they'd sent Jesse the night before to check on the cattle there. If he'd been hurt and lay on the ground, they could spend hours locating him. Tufts of prairie grass sprang up everywhere. He could be down in a gully, having been thrown by his horse after a particularly loud clash of thunder.

For the moment, Reed held on to hope and Mona. She smelled of rain and citrus. Despite spending the night in a cave and being drenched and muddy, she still made him hot. Her beauty went beyond the exterior package. She cared about her home and her people, wearing her heart for all to see. Unashamed and brave.

His arms tightened high around her waist, between the baby bump and her breasts. She loved with a fierceness Reed had not witnessed and she'd love her baby as deeply.

He fought the strange stab of envy stirring in his gut. How would it feel to be loved with such conviction?

Thoughts of love and the baby fled his mind when the sound of a dog's howling reached his ears over the pounding of the horse's hooves. "Stop!" he yelled into Mona's ear.

She pulled back so hard, the horse reared.

Reed knew holding too tightly to Mona wasn't an

option, so he let go and slid down the horse's rump to land on his bottom on the damp earth already steaming in the morning sun.

Trailing Mona, Fernando almost ran over Reed, his horse's hooves narrowly missing Reed's hands.

Mona fought to calm the horse, pulling it in a circle until it came to a standstill. Then she turned to Reed. "Are you all right?"

"I'm fine." He picked himself up off the ground and brushed the mud from his jeans. "I thought I heard a dog—"

Another howl rose in the air from somewhere in the vicinity of a dip in the landscape two hundred yards ahead.

Mona stared at Fernando. "Chewy?"

He nodded and they kicked their mounts at the same time, sending them loping toward the sound and leaving Reed to make the trek on foot.

The two riders disappeared into a gully.

Reed increased his pace until he was running, his heart thundering against his chest. What if one of the rustlers had set a trap? What if the howling dog wasn't Chewy but a rabid coyote?

When he reached the banks of the gully, his lungs were bursting inside his chest.

Mona crouched in the dirt beside a still form, her ear pressed against it. The black-and-white border collie nudged the lump of rags and raised his snout to the sky, sending up a sad and lonely howl.

"Is it Jesse?" Reed asked as he scrambled down the banks into the muddy gulch.

"*Sí.*" Fernando held his hat in his hands, his brown eyes sad.

"Is he alive?" Reed dropped to his knees and reached for the man's throat to feel for a pulse.

"I think so. I can hear his heartbeat and he's breathing. Barely. We have to get him to a hospital." Mona stared at his shredded clothing and the scrapes on his face and hands. "What could have happened to cause all that?"

Reed stood, the muscle in his jaw twitching. He nodded toward the rope burns around Jesse's wrists. "He was dragged across the prairie. Probably by the four-wheelers that chased us."

Mona's face paled and she staggered to her feet. "Damn it!"

Jesse stirred, his eyelids fluttering open. Through cracked lips he croaked out, "Chewy bit one of them on the hand. Pretty bad."

MONA COULD BARELY control the anger burbling up inside her. She'd stayed with Jesse while Fernando rode back to the ranch and called for an Air Life helicopter to lift Jesse to the hospital in Amarillo.

It was one thing to target her ranch and the cattle. But after Catalina and Jesse had been hurt, she was madder than hell and determined to put a stop to all the bloodshed.

A careful search yielded some of the stolen cattle, scattered across her uncle's ranch. Apparently the storm and the mud scared the rustlers into aborting their mission. She'd deal with the loose cattle when she could. Fernando made the call to her uncle to buy time until they could get out there and bring them back over the fence line.

The thought of mending more fences made her want to drop into a chair and cry. The lightning strike that knocked out the electricity had also fried her computer. They hadn't been able to log on to the tracking Web site to check the cattle locations.

Mona groaned. Would the work ever lessen? Would the problems ever go away? Hell, no. But some problems seemed too big for her to handle.

She paced the wooden floor of her father's study, unsure of her next move, but determined not to fail. She'd called the state police, but they'd referred her to local law enforcement. Did someone she cared about have to die before they did anything?

Reed leaned against the door frame, his brows raised. "You should sit and give that baby some rest."

"We have to stop this, Reed. I just don't know how." She paced across the floor and back to stand in front of him. "Do I have to sell my ranch to keep others from getting hurt?"

"You're not selling your ranch. We need to find someone who's been bitten recently by a dog and follow his boss back to the source of all this trouble."

Mona snorted. "Yeah, like whoever it was will just show off his dog bite to us and the police." She wrapped her arms around her belly and stared up at the ceiling. "We could start by calling all the local hospitals and emergency clinics to see if someone came in with a dog bite."

Reed shook his head. "Only if he wants to be caught. More likely, he'll tend to his wound himself. This area isn't that populated, but a man could easily hide in the hundreds of empty acres spread out across the panhandle."

"This can't go on. That man at the granary was killed, probably for what he knew. Jesse was left for dead. Who else will die before we catch the rustlers?" Mona paced the room again, the color high in her cheekbones, her brown eyes flashing. "What about the four-wheelers?"

"What about them?" Reed pushed a hand through his hair. "Most ranchers have them."

"The eighteen-wheeler. Surely you can't hide a truck that big." Mona's gaze narrowed. "And what happened to the rider that fell back down the ravine? Don't you think his bike got wrecked? Maybe he was injured."

"Apparently the four-wheeler wasn't damaged enough to keep him from getting it out of the canyon. As for the tractor-trailer rig, there are plenty of truck stops in the area with cattle trailers. This area is the beef capital of Texas. Chances are slim of finding it."

"But it would be covered in mud up to the axles."

"They could have cleaned it by now." He grabbed her shoulders and looked down at her.

Her eyes pooled with tears, her lips pursed in a thin line that trembled. "What *can* we do?"

REED'S HEART SQUEEZED in his chest and he bent to kiss her forehead. "It wouldn't hurt to go look for the rig." He kissed the tip of her nose and finally her lips. He knew he was wrong, but he couldn't resist. She looked so hopeless and sad.

When Mona's lips parted, Reed thrust through, taking her tongue with his. His fingers wound through her long black hair, the silken strands reminding him of how she'd felt curled against him in the cave, the scent of citrus wafting to his nostrils, making him hard all over.

Her hands crept up his chest, bunching his shirt in her fists, tugging him closer, deepening the kiss. When their lips parted, she stared into his eyes, her own going wide. "I shouldn't have done that." She pushed against him and he let her go. With her back to him she rubbed her hands down the sides of her jeans.

Dogs barked outside the window.

Reed and Mona stepped out onto the porch as two vehicles pulled into the yard. Fernando's farm truck carrying Catalina and Rosa, and her uncle's truck.

Mona closed her eyes and took a deep breath. "Great. Who invited him?"

Rosa helped Catalina down from the truck and across the yard to the house.

"How are you, sweetie?" Mona cupped her friend's cheek.

"I'm okay. I could have left the hospital a lot sooner but for the doctor. I think he liked me." She winked, then her expression became serious. "It's you I'm worried about." When her mother edged Catalina toward the door, she dug in her heels. "No way I'm missing this shoot-out with Uncle Arty. I'll just sit in the rocker for a ringside seat."

Mona rolled her eyes and smiled. "You really should rest."

Catalina waved her concern away and settled into the rocker. "Later. I really do feel much better."

"Mona, what in tarnation is going on?" Uncle Arty stomped up the porch steps. "I came as soon as your foreman called about your cattle all over my place."

"My foreman has a name. It's Fernando." Mona's back stiffened. "And you tell me, Uncle, what's going on?"

Reed suppressed a smile. For the past half an hour, Mona had struggled with what to do, her body sagging with the effort. But as soon as the questions began, her strength seemed to return.

"What to you mean? You don't think *I* had anything to do with the rustling, do you?" Arty blustered.

Mona walked up to the older man and stood toe-to-toe with him. "Then why did they stage it on your property?"

Arty Grainger backed up a step, a frown pulling his bushy white brows together. "Perhaps because it was closer to the road than yours. Did you think of that?"

"All I know is that I've been robbed, shot at and almost killed in the past few days. I've even been accused of a murder I did not commit. The only person I can think of who hates me enough to make my life miserable is you. Tell me, where were you during all this?"

Reed stepped forward, wanting to tell her that her uncle had come up with her bail money, even though he'd made Reed swear not to tell. A stern stare from Mr. Grainger made him bite his lip and let the conversation take its course.

Mona was on a roll. She took a deep breath, lowering her voice, although the intensity deepened. "You've wanted me to fail at ranching even more than you wanted my father to. Do you deny it?"

Uncle Arty stared at her for a moment before answering. "No, I don't deny it. And I was wrong. But I was never involved in the rustling. I promise."

"After giving my father hell for years, you expect me to believe you?" She turned her back. "Go away. I can handle this on my own."

"That's just it. You're the only one with the rustler problems."

Mona faced her uncle again. "Just me?"

"Yeah. None of the other ranches are getting hit. Someone…" Her uncle shook his head. "Someone has it in for you, Mona."

"Why me?"

"I don't know. Although I wanted you to fail at the ranch, I didn't want anyone to get hurt. I never wanted you or your father to get hurt. I just wanted Grainger land to remain intact. That's all I ever wanted. I even hired Dusty to keep an eye on you and report in every week on what was going on over here."

"You hired Dusty?"

Her uncle snorted. "You don't think he came to work here because of the great pay, do you?"

"You hired Dusty to spy on me?" Mona's face flamed. "I should have known."

"Listen, I came to help in any way I can."

"By hiring spies? I think not."

"I told you, I was wrong about you and about Dusty. I think he might have something to do with the rustling. If I could buy his information, who's to say he didn't sell it to others? Not to mention, he's been wearing more expensive clothing out on the town and driving a new pickup."

"The bastard." Mona's mouth firmed into a tight line.

Stepping forward, Reed cupped Mona's elbow. "Makes sense, Mona. We should check it out."

She stared up at her uncle, betrayal making her

eyes glassy with unshed tears. "I'd expect as much from Dusty, but you were family."

Arty nodded. "I'm sorry to say, but I'd bet my last dollar Dusty is involved in the rustling."

She stared out at the rain-washed horizon. "Why didn't I see it?"

"Because you were busy. He drove an old beat-up truck to work every day and did what you told him, for the most part." Reed wanted to take her in his arms, instead he stayed back. She wouldn't want to show any weakness in front of her uncle.

"If it makes you feel any better, your father didn't know either."

She faced her uncle, her brows rising up her forehead. "That's supposed to make me feel better? Your spying on your own brother is supposed to make this all right?" She crossed to her uncle. "Get out."

"Now, Mona. I said I was sorry and I am. I came to help."

"I don't need your help. I don't need any man's help. Not now or ever. I'll figure this out on my own. Now get out before I call the sheriff to have you thrown out."

Mona marched back into the house, leaving Reed, Catalina and Arty standing on the porch.

Reed shrugged. "You can't expect her to trust you after so many years."

"I know. I just wish I'd done things differently before her father died." Then he descended the porch stairs and left.

Mona pushed through the screen door, letting it slam behind her. Her keys jangled from her fingers as she crossed the porch and took the steps downward two at a time.

"Where are you going?" Reed asked.

"To town." She climbed into the driver's seat of the pickup and started the engine.

"Don't just stand there, go get her," Catalina said.

Reed barely had time to leap from the porch to the ground and round the pickup, before she backed out. "Let me go with you."

She ignored him, braking to a halt, the truck skidding in the gravel.

Before she could shift into drive, he grabbed the door handle, flung it open and threw himself onto the passenger seat.

Her foot hit the accelerator before his door was closed, the truck fishtailing down the driveway. She was hell-bent on getting herself killed and taking everyone down who stood in the way.

Reed slammed his door and buckled his seat belt. He was in for a helluva ride.

Chapter Twelve

Mona slammed her hand against the steering wheel, the truck veering onto the shoulder before she straightened it. "How could I be so blind?"

"You trust people." Reed held on to the handle above the door, his gaze flicking from the road to her. "There's no crime in trusting people."

"Apparently there is." Despite her anger, Mona was glad he'd insisted on coming with her. "For that matter, why should I trust you?" She glared at him.

"You probably shouldn't." His sad smile did nothing to calm her.

In fact it made her madder. How could he sit in that seat looking so damn handsome she could barely keep her eyes on the road? "Why are you still working for me? Other men would have quit at the first sign of trouble. What makes you different?"

"I guess you could say I have a habit of sticking up for the underdog."

"Now you're comparing me to a dog?" She

laughed, only the sound came out as more of a snort. "I'm flattered."

"Slow down and, while you're at it, quit twisting my words." He tightened his grip on the handle, all evidence of his smile wiped away when she took the turn off the ranch road onto the pavement too fast.

If not for the seat belt, he'd have been slung across the seat into her. Mona almost regretted the fully functional seat belts.

"By the way, where are we going?" he asked.

"Dusty's place. I have a bone to pick with the man."

"Oh no you're not." Before she could pick up speed, Reed reached over and switched the ignition key to the off position.

How dare he? Mona shifted the truck into neutral and switched it back on. "Don't do that. You could have gotten us killed."

"And you could get us killed. If Dusty is the one who dragged Jesse around the central pasture and shot the Mexican at the granary, you could be walking into an explosive situation."

"I have a baby to think about. I won't do anything stupid." She stared across at Reed. "I have to know."

"Why don't you take it to the sheriff?"

Mona snorted. "He's as worthless as teats on a billy goat."

Reed laughed out loud. "I've never heard Parker referred to as…well, anyway. If you can't take it to Parker, let me handle it."

"I won't stand by and let him get away with hurting the people I care about, damn it." Were those tears blurring her vision? She swiped at her eyes. "Damn hormones. Really, I never cry. In fact, I've never thought like a female before in my life."

"I believe you. Maybe now's the time you should. Your baby needs your love and protection. Pull over."

They'd already reached the outskirts of Prairie Rock where the density of the houses was greater the farther into town they drove.

Should she let him handle it? Mona slowed and turned right on Third Street. "Too late, we're here."

The dingy white clapboard house was almost as small as the shed out back of Mona's ranch house. The screen door hung lopsided on one hinge and the paint curled off the wooden door frame. Old metal chairs littered the front yard, along with worn tires and a pair of broken sawhorses. In the gravel driveway sat the old truck Mona recognized as the one Dusty drove to her house every day. No lights shone from inside and the tattered blinds were drawn.

"Suppose he's home?" She sat behind the wheel, not at all anxious to get out, now that they were here. What would she say to Dusty when she confronted him? *Did you kill the Mexican? Did you almost kill Jesse? Are you stealing my cattle?* What did she expect as an answer? He'd deny everything and where would that leave her? Accusing him of something she couldn't prove. "We need evidence."

"Of what?"

"Cattle rustling, connections with whoever owns the truck. Something, anything." She stared around the other houses in the neighborhood. Most were boarded up or run-down with broken windows staring like ghosts at the once-lively street. "I can't just park here if we're going to look around."

"So now you're going to spy on Dusty?" Reed shook his head. "No way."

She pressed her foot to the gas pedal and sent the truck shooting forward and around to the next block. A small overgrown field afforded a wide area to pull off the road. She shoved the truck into park and climbed down. Without waiting for Reed to follow, she tramped across weed-infested yards back over to Third Street and Dusty Gaither's house.

"I really wish you'd reconsider," Reed said, running to catch up to her. "You're in no condition to be playing detective."

"If Dusty *is* involved, I need enough evidence to get the police to take me seriously."

"Then let me do this." He grabbed her hand and pulled her up against him. "Please, Mona, go back to the truck and wait."

Pressed hard against Reed's chest, Mona couldn't breathe, not because he held her too tightly, but because she couldn't breathe when she was this close to the man. "Reed, you don't understand. I can't go back. These are my people, my home, my ranch being threatened. If this was your family, would you turn your back on them?"

Reed stiffened and he drew away from her. "You're right. I don't understand."

"We may not have much time. If we want to look through his things, we need to do it and get out before he comes home. Are you with me, or not?" She stared at him for a long time. She was asking him to break the law, something he used to be a part of. Was that fair? "Never mind. I'm already in trouble with the law, just stand guard and warn me if someone drives up." With that she turned on her booted heels and strode across the street.

Before she'd gone two yards, Reed caught up with her again and moved ahead. "If anyone is going to break the law, it'll be me."

Mona admired the way his muscles rippled beneath the tight jersey knit of his black T-shirt. Hatless, his blond hair shone with red and gold highlights glinting across the short waves. In the daylight, she could finally see some of what her fingers had explored the night before and her body heated all the way to her core.

With a forcible shake, she pulled her head out of the desire threatening to derail her efforts and hurried to keep up with the man knocking on Dusty's front door.

AFTER THE FOURTH KNOCK, Reed concluded Dusty Gaither wasn't home. With a quick glance around at the deserted neighborhood, he hurried around the back of the building, Mona close on his heels. He wished she'd gone back to the truck. He didn't like the idea of her getting caught breaking the law. She'd be back in jail in a flash and her lawyer and connections could do nothing to bail her out again.

The backyard was even junkier than the front, with an old engine dangling by a chain from a tree, a rusty washing machine on its side in a stand of weeds hip high. The trash can by the back door overflowed with pizza boxes and beer bottles. Reed went straight for the can. A man's garbage told a lot about the man. He tossed the pizza boxes to the ground, followed quickly by newspapers and beer bottles.

Without questioning, Mona dug into the mess, pulling out hamburger wrappers and papers.

"It can't be good for your baby to be going through trash."

"You're more worried than a mother hen about this baby." She didn't stop what she was doing, all but turning upside down to get to the bottom stack of old bills and soda cans. "I promise to wash my hands when we're done." When she straightened, she frowned at the papers she'd found. "Looks like a credit-card bill and a bank statement."

"Let me see." Reed leaned over her shoulder and stared down at the food-smeared documents. "He likes to spend money, doesn't he?"

"Yeah, more than what he made at Rancho Linda."

"Looks like more than what he made at both the ranch and what your uncle paid him." He pointed at a charge for a thirty-six-inch plasma television set at the electronics store down in Amarillo.

"Whew, look at the balance." Mona's eyes widened. "Over fifteen thousand dollars."

"Our man Dusty is in way over his head."

"Look at this." Mona held up a past-due notice from the local utilities company and another from a financial institution listing a loan for a new truck.

"Looks like he likes to spend money he doesn't have." Reed dug around in the last of the trash and started putting it all back into the can. "It's a motive, but it's not enough."

"We need to get inside." Mona reached for the rusty handle to the back screen door.

"Not we." Reed removed her hand from the handle and stared down at her. "Stay outside and warn me if he drives up." He tipped her chin upward and stared down into her liquid brown eyes. "Please."

Her teeth bit into her bottom lip, making Reed want to kiss it. Finally she let it go and nodded. "Okay. But hurry, will you?"

He bent and acted on his urge, pressing a kiss to her lips. "I will." Expecting to have to pry the lock, he was amazed when the wood-paneled door opened and swung inward just by turning the knob, making breaking and entering much easier.

Reed moved through the kitchen, noting the

ancient sink and cabinets that must have been there since the early fifties. Rust stains ringed the sink drain and the vinyl floors peeled up around the edges.

He pulled the drawers open, quickly moving through the kitchen without finding anything worth clueing in on. In the tiny living area, a massive television stood in the corner, blocking most of the window. A sofa with missing cushions and a crocheted blanket thrown over the back looked as if it had been lived in by rats. Beer bottles littered the rickety coffee table and the threadbare rug. The place reeked of stale beer, old shoes and filth.

On an end table, buried beneath the television guide and dog-eared copies of *Sports Illustrated*, Reed found a bank statement.

"Find something useful?"

Reed spun, dropping into a fighting stance before he realized the voice in his ear was Mona's. "I thought you said you'd play lookout."

"Figured I could hear a vehicle from inside as well as outside, given how old the house is and the fact it probably isn't well insulated."

"Still, I'd feel better if you waited outside."

She tilted her head to the side, her eyes going wide. "Too late."

Reed froze, his ears picking up the sound of an engine headed their way. "Quick. Out the back door."

"Can't." Mona ducked to peer out the window. "He's pulling around that way." She ran for the front door, but the door was jammed shut. "Shootfire, it won't open."

"Come on." Reed grabbed her hand and raced into a tiny bathroom. He shoved her into the claw-foot tub, surrounded by an ancient shower curtain hanging by its last five intact rings, and climbed in beside her. "How can I keep you safe if you refuse to do what I say?"

"No one tells me what to do, cowboy. Haven't you figured that out yet?" She shot him a crooked smile about the time the back screen door opened and slammed shut. Booted feet clomped through the house into the bedroom, where dresser drawers were opened and slammed shut. A door banged open and closed with enough force to rattle the bathroom walls.

Mona jumped, clamping a hand over her mouth.

Reed circled her waist, resting his palms over her baby bump, gently pulling her against his chest.

The stiffness in her shoulders relaxed only slightly, but she leaned against him, her hands coming up to cover his. He liked it.

Too much. Inhaling the scent of her hair almost made him forget the compromising position they were in, standing in Gaither's tub.

"Hey." Dusty's voice, muffled by the thickness of the walls. "I need more money. Meet me behind the bank in five minutes or I'll let the cat out of the bag." The plastic crack of a phone hitting the cradle carried through the walls. "Stupid son of a—" Footsteps moved toward the small bathroom.

Reed held his breath and Mona's wrist. Her pulse beat like a runaway metronome.

The toilet lid clattered against the tank and the sound of liquid spraying into water was accompanied by the sharp odor of urine.

Mona's belly clenched and her hand moved to cover her mouth and nose.

The rasp of a zipper was followed by footfalls and Dusty left the bathroom and the house, the screen door slamming behind him.

"He didn't even flush or wash his hands." Mona stumbled out of the bath and into the living room.

Reed followed, checking out the kitchen window to see Dusty's truck pulling out of the driveway. "Come on." Reed grabbed her hand and ran out the back door and to the street. When Dusty's truck disappeared around the corner, Reed ran across the road and through the neglected yards of the abandoned houses.

Mona pulled her hand free of his and stopped, bending double, her face creased in pain. "Go on without me."

Guilt hit him in the chest like a tight knot. He'd forgotten for a moment that Mona couldn't run as fast as he could in her condition. He slid to a halt and hurried back to her. "Are you all right? No labor pains or anything?"

"No, just a stitch in my side. I'll be fine as soon as

I catch my breath. In the meantime Dusty's getting away. Go on. I'll be fine. I can walk downtown to Dee's Diner and wait for you there."

Reed shook his head. "I won't leave you."

As she straightened, Mona forced a smile, her face tight. "See? I'm fine. Now go on." Then she doubled over again, clutching her side. "Damn!"

Reed scooped her into his arms and carried her to the truck as though she were no heavier than a sack of feed.

"You can't go carrying me around everywhere, you know." Mona's lips pressed into a tight line and the arm around his shoulder remained stiff. "You're going to miss who Dusty is meeting with."

Reed eased her onto the truck seat and buckled her in before going around to the driver's seat. "I think we need to take you to the hospital."

"If you aren't going to follow Dusty, move over so that I can drive." She started to unbuckle her seat belt.

"I'll drive." But he wasn't too happy about it. He glanced at Mona several times along the short trip to the town square where the bank was located.

Mona glared at him. "Stop staring at me. I'm not going to break. Where the heck is he?"

When neither Dusty nor his truck could be found on the square, Reed circled the block behind the bank and crept down the street, trying to catch glimpses of the alleyway between the businesses and the bank. "There." He stopped and pointed at the dark metallic gray pickup parked in front of Daisy's Florist Shop. Dusty wasn't in the truck. Reed pulled around the corner and parked. "Stay here. Do you understand? If you follow me, I'll personally carry you back to the truck and all the way to Amarillo to the hospital."

"You can't do that. It would be kidnapping." Mona crossed her arms over her chest. "I want to see who he's meeting as well as you do."

"Who's to say you won't get another stitch in your side?" He gave her a stern look and appealed to her in another way. "You could slow me down."

Her dark brows arrowed downward. "Okay. But hurry. I have to pee."

A smile curved his lips as he climbed down from the truck and entered the alley behind a building farther away from the bank. He peered around the corner of the building and spied Dusty facing the back of the bank, apparently talking to someone standing in the back door. Dusty didn't look happy, his voice rising.

"I need more. Either you give me twenty thousand or I go to the newspaper with the story."

Another voice murmured in low tones Reed couldn't hear. Who was it? Easing around a Dumpster, he worked his way closer to the pair in the alley.

"You'll pay one way or another," Dusty said.

Reed stepped around a stack of cardboard boxes with flower petals and leaves clinging to them. Just as he was about to lean around another Dumpster, he must have nudged the stack. A dozen boxes toppled over.

On the other side of the Dumpster, Dusty muttered, "Damn." He made a break for an alley, cutting through to the street where he'd parked his truck.

Leaping over the fallen boxes, Reed landed in the middle of the alley in time to see Dusty disappear between buildings.

Reed raced after him. As he passed the back door to the bank, the door slammed shut. Pausing long enough to grab the door handle, he tried to open it to see who was behind it. The door was locked.

If he got to Dusty, he might wring a few answers out of him. When he emerged on the street where Dusty was parked, the other man had already backed out of his parking space. Reed ran out in front of the truck.

Dusty didn't stop. He shoved the shift into drive and raced toward Reed.

With only inches to spare, Reed dived to the side, hitting the pavement and rolling out of the way of the truck's wheels. By the time he leaped to his feet, Dusty had rounded the corner, squealing tires leaving a long trail of black rubber burned into the pavement.

His only hope of catching Dusty was to get to his truck quickly. Reed ran to the end of the street and turned the corner. Only his truck stood there. Empty. Where was Mona?

MONA NEVER CLAIMED to be good at waiting. After two torturous minutes, she gave up and climbed down from the truck. She couldn't go after Reed without possibly alerting Dusty to his presence.

Since Dusty was meeting someone behind the bank, what could it hurt to go inside the bank to see who was moving around? She could go in on the pretense of speaking with Mr. Kuhn about foreclosing on the loan. Maybe even try begging for a change. Anger and disbelief hadn't done a thing for her. It galled her to consider getting on her knees to save her ranch. But hadn't she said she'd do anything to protect her child's heritage? So eating a little crow couldn't be too bad.

She tugged her shirt, the long tails draping down almost to her knees. Before too long someone was going to wise up and notice she was preggers. Word would get back to Sheriff Parker and she'd be in the custody battle to end all custody battles. She really had to stop coming to town. But first, to find the low-down, sons of a gun preying on her ranch.

Mona pushed through the glass doors and stepped into the cool bank lobby. Two tellers smiled at her. The first one, Doris Liehman spoke. "Good afternoon, Miss Grainger. What can I do for you today?"

"Is Mr. Kuhn available? I'd like to speak with him."

"Let me check." Doris stepped around the counter and crossed the tiled floor to the hallway leading into the back office area.

Mona followed and waited while Doris knocked on Mr. Kuhn's door. She waited and knocked again.

Finally, she opened the door and peered inside and then closed the door. "I'm sorry, he's not in his office right now. He was here just a minute ago. If you'll have a seat in the lobby, I'm sure he'll be right back. Or I could leave a message."

"I have a few minutes. I'll wait." Mona eyed the end of the hallway that led to the bank's back door. Only employees could go in and out of the back door. Was Mr. Kuhn the man Dusty was meeting outside in the alley? If so, why?

Doris returned to her teller window with an apologetic smile.

Mona took a seat in the lobby that afforded her a view of the hallway and the back door. She didn't have to wait long.

Kuhn practically leaped in through the door, locking it behind him. Okay, this was interesting. What business did Kuhn have with the likes of Dusty Gaither?

Mona leaned back, out of sight of the hallway, and gave Mr. Kuhn time to make it to his office, before she stood and walked back.

Without knocking, she entered his office and closed the door behind her quietly.

Apparently, Mr. Kuhn didn't hear the door open or close. He stood with his back to her, staring out his window at the brick building next to the bank.

Mona cleared her throat.

Mr. Kuhn swung around, his eyes wide. "How the hell did you get in here?"

Feigning innocence, Mona motioned toward the door. "The normal way. I need to discuss things with you."

His eyes narrowed and he glanced down at his watch. "I'm sorry, but I have an appointment in exactly two minutes."

"I'm sure it can wait." Mona stalked across the floor and stood in front of Kuhn's desk. "Why is it that when I went to apply to another bank for a loan, I discover my credit has been ruined?"

A mask dropped down over Kuhn's face, his green eyes hardening to look like granite. "I have no idea. It's your credit rating, not mine."

"Seems this bank has indicated I've been late paying my loan payments every month for the past year." Mona crossed her arms over her chest. "How can that be when I get them to you early?"

"Credit-reporting tools aren't infallible."

"Yeah." Mona seethed inwardly. She'd suspected it when he'd informed her that the bank was foreclosing on her, but now she had her proof. Kuhn was trying to force her into selling her property or taking it as collateral in a foreclosure. "Bastard."

"If you'll excuse me, I have another appointment." Kuhn walked around the desk and to the door.

"Why do you want Rancho Linda? What's so special about it that you'd ruin me to get it?"

"I don't know what you're talking about. Now please leave before I call the sheriff."

"Tell me this, then." Mona walked up to Kuhn and stood toe to toe with the son of a bitch who'd ruin a lone female rancher without batting an eyelash. "Are you and Dusty Gaither behind the cattle rustling?"

A muscle in Kuhn's jaw twitched, but his eyes remained cold. "I have nothing to do with the cattle rustling or Dusty Gaither."

"And if I take it to the police, I'm sure they'll prove that."

"Absolutely. Now leave before I call the sheriff." He opened the door and held it for her.

Mona stepped into the door frame, but not through. "I think it's time I get a lawyer. Perhaps you'd better do the same." She turned to leave and stopped, twisting around. "Oh, and just so you know, I'd sell to my uncle Arty before I'd ever consider selling to an oil speculator."

As she left the bank, two men in suits entered. The same men who'd been at the diner the other day when she'd met with Catalina. The men she'd said were oil brokers. Mona turned and stared at their backs as Doris led them into Kuhn's office.

Was that it? Was he after her land for the oil? Oh yeah, she was definitely calling her lawyer as soon as possible. She hurried back to the truck to inform Reed of what she'd learned.

When she turned the corner, she practically ran headfirst into him.

His face was stormy and he grabbed her arms. "Where have you been? I thought I told you to stay put."

"I had business to conduct." As close as he stood, she could smell the soap on his skin, and the light musk of pure male. Her stomach fluttered, her body heating at his touch.

His hands tightened on her arms in an almost bruising grip, before he dropped them, shaking his head. "You're killing me, Grainger."

"Better me than someone else." Ignoring the warmth spreading throughout her body, Mona hurried to the truck, climbing into the driver's seat. "We have work to do."

Reed slipped into the passenger's side.

Before his door was fully closed, she shifted the truck in reverse and pulled out into the street.

"Where did you go?"

She shrugged. "I had business at the bank."

Reed closed his eyes and counted to ten. "And what did you find out?"

"You first." Mona cast him an amused smile. "I promise I'll tell if you tell."

"Dusty met with someone at the back door to the bank."

Mona nodded. "Mr. Kuhn."

"How do you know?"

"I was in the bank when Kuhn came rushing in the back door like a scalded cat."

"Tell me you didn't confront him." Reed looked

over at her, his eyes narrowing when she didn't answer immediately. "You didn't, did you?"

"I told you, I had business. I met with Mr. Kuhn about my loan." She turned a corner a little faster than she should, the back two wheels slipping across pavement, sending up an ear-splitting screech.

"You confronted him." Reed shook his head. "What do I have to do, tie you up to keep you from hurting yourself?"

Mona grinned. "That idea has promise."

When he didn't laugh, she sighed. "Kuhn has screwed up my credit. He's still threatening to fore-close and take Rancho Linda. I more or less accused him of being behind the rustling efforts with Dusty Gaither."

Reed's brows shot upward. "And?"

She shrugged. "He denied it, of course."

"Did he say anything about his meeting with Dusty?"

"He said he didn't have anything to do with Dusty."

Reed looked around at the street she turned down. "Where are you going?"

"I think my truck needs a bit of bodywork. Les and Wayne's body shop is just the place." She pulled into the gravel parking lot in front of a dilapidated building. Rolled-up overhead doors gaped open, exposing the interior clutter of old car doors, bumpers and fenders.

Mona climbed down from the pickup studying the two trucks parked in front of the body shop, one new and shiny, the other beat-up and dented. Wrecked cars flanked the sides of the building, grease spots stained the ground and grubby prints adorned the door frames. Why had Les and Wayne been talking with the Mexicans? Oscar the bartender had mentioned seeing them together.

"Are you thinking Les and Wayne had something to do with the shooting at the granary?" Reed stared across at her.

Mona shrugged. "Don't worry. I won't do anything to endanger myself and the baby. I'm here on business."

She detected shadowy movements inside the shop, maybe two people, but she couldn't make them out. Wayne Fennel worked here along with Les Newton. The beauty of a small town. Everyone knew everyone else and where they belonged.

With a deep breath and determined steps, Mona met Reed at the front right fender and pretended to study the dent that had been there since well before her father died, but suddenly needed fixing.

Wayne strutted out, dressed in his signature starched blue jeans and shiny cowboy boots, reeking of cheap cologne and stale cigarettes. "Afternoon, Mona. What brings you into town?" His tone, open and friendly, didn't exactly match the narrowed eyes.

Mona forced a friendly smile and stuck out her hand to Wayne. "Thought I'd get an estimate on what it would take to fix my front bumper. Been meaning to for a long time."

He took her hand, his gaze sweeping her from head to foot, coming back to the deep valley of her breasts, peeking out of the cotton button-up shirt she'd chosen to wear that morning.

Reed stepped forward, blocking Wayne's view. "So what do you think about the bumper?" Tight-lipped, his tone and hard glare was enough to shake Wayne's mind out of the cleavage and back to the truck repairs.

Her stomach churning, Mona fought back the bile rising in her throat. Having Wayne touch her hand and stare at her like she was a naked woman in a porn magazine made her want to gag. And if he had anything to do with the rustling, God help him.

"Well, let's see." Wayne stared down at the bumper and scratched his head. "I'll have to work up an estimate."

"I've got a few minutes, I'll wait." Mona walked toward the shop. "I could do with a soda." She fished in her pockets for change, all the while scanning the darker interior of the body shop.

"We got a lot of cars ahead of you. I don't think I can get to it until sometime next week." He followed her, his boots slipping in the gravel as he scrambled to catch up.

"That's okay, I just want an estimate. Not sure the old truck is worth fixin'. Knowing what it'll take might help me make that decision." She counted out the change she needed for the faded soda machine outside the office door. "Les around? Haven't seen much of him lately."

Reed leaned against the overhead door frame. "I hear Les does good work. I might have a job he can do for me. Where is he?"

"Les called in sick." Wayne stepped into the dirty office area where papers littered the desktop, held down by a ball-hitch paperweight.

His office smelled of grease, oil and cigarettes. An ashtray overflowed with spent butts.

The stench turned Mona's delicate stomach. She shot a glance at Reed and blocked the doorway with her body, giving Reed a chance to slip inside the shop and have a look around. "That's too bad. I hope it isn't contagious. Hate to see you get whatever he's got."

"Oh, it's not contagious." Wayne grabbed a pen and estimate worksheet. "Just the bumper?" His glance shot over her shoulder through the doorway.

"I don't know. Could you work up an estimate on the tailgate as well? I dropped a round bale on it, which snapped the retaining wires."

Wayne scratched on the paper. Nothing came out of the pen. He slammed the pen in the trash and dug in the desk drawer for another. "Front bumper and tailgate. Year, model?"

Mona gave him the details and he wrote the information down in a hurry, then stood. "I'll have to make calls about the tailgate and get back to you on the estimate. You can call back tomorrow."

Mona stood in the doorway, her body tense, blocking Wayne's escape. "Pretty wicked storm last night, huh?"

"I guess. Didn't notice."

"You weren't out in it, were you?"

Wayne looked at her through slitted eyes. "I said I didn't notice." He took the three steps that positioned him directly in front of Mona. "Why do you ask?"

With Wayne towering over her, Mona wasn't feeling so brave all of a sudden. She stepped out of the office and turned to where Reed had been leaning against the overhead door leading into the shop. He wasn't there. Her heart skipped several beats before slamming into fast gear. She spun back toward Wayne. "I was wondering, you wouldn't happen to know where I could get a good used four-wheeler, would you?"

He shrugged, his shoulders stiff, the muscle in his jaw twitching. "Wouldn't know. Look in the Amarillo newspapers."

"I have, but it's hard to find one you can trust. Funny. Isn't that the way with a lot of things nowadays?" With nothing left to say, and Wayne being less than forthcoming with his previous evening's activities, Mona had no choice but to leave the shop. Where was Reed? "I'll come by tomorrow for that estimate."

"Don't bother, just call." Once she'd moved through the doorway, he stepped around her, his gaze panning the interior of the shop. "Where'd your boyfriend go?"

Chapter Thirteen

Reed hadn't liked leaving Mona in the office with Wayne. But in broad daylight, with Mona acting as if she had legitimate business with the man, Wayne shouldn't try anything, as long as Mona didn't ask too many questions.

For a split second, a flash of panic surged through Reed and he almost turned back. No. She wouldn't be stupid.

And they really didn't have a viable reason to believe Wayne and Les were involved in the rustling. All they had to go on was the bartender's observations.

After his eyes adjusted to the dark interior, Reed hadn't seen anything damning in the shop that would link Wayne and Les to Dusty and cattle rustling. With casual ease, he'd walked back out in the sunshine, wind whipping dust into his eyes. Just as nonchalantly, he'd circled the back of the building, his hands in his pockets as if he was bored, waiting on the boss lady. Once around the side and out of sight, he'd sprinted to the end of the building and peered around back into the junkyard of old cars and spare parts.

A movement caught his eye. At first he thought it was a rat. In a way, he'd been right. Les Newton moved among the rusty hulls of old cars, ducking low to remain out of sight, staring at the back door of the building.

Reed had stood still to avoid detection until Les stepped out into the open. At that moment, Reed's blood ran cold.

Les's right hand was wrapped in a flesh-colored bandage.

The thought of Mona in the office alone with Wayne sent a blast of fear through Reed.

When Les had his back to him, Reed eased around the side of the building, and moved to the front, just as Mona stepped out of Wayne's office. Reed entered the shop from the direction of the truck and hooked Mona's arm with his hand.

She jumped, her eyes wide until she realized it was him.

"Ready to go?" he asked.

She sucked in a deep breath and let it out before she turned a brilliant smile on him. "Yes. I'm ready." Her voice shook, but she turned a confident expression toward Wayne. "Thanks. I'll expect that estimate tomorrow."

As the truck pulled out of the gravel parking area, Wayne stood by the door. Watching.

Mona waved through the rolled-up window. "What did you find?" she said through her smile.

Reed gunned the accelerator, sending the truck shooting out onto the highway. "Les didn't call in sick."

Her gaze shot to Reed's profile. "What do you mean?"

"He was hiding in back of the shop."

"Why?"

His jaw tight, Reed stared over at the woman beside him. "Probably had something to do with the bandage on his hand."

Mona's deep-brown gaze locked with his. "You think he was the one bitten by the dog?"

Reed nodded.

"Finally!" She clapped her hands together, her smile lighting the interior of the cab. "We have proof. Let's go to the sheriff with this information. He can arrest them and be done with it." Her head swung around as they passed the sheriff's office without slowing. "Why didn't you stop? Pull over."

"Think about it, Mona. Do you really believe Wayne and Les have the intelligence and where-withal to pull off this big of an operation?"

"They might not be the sharpest individuals Prairie Rock has to offer but, for now, they're the only ones we know are involved in the rustling."

"Someone with more influence and financial support has to be leading this effort. Until we find him, arresting Les and Wayne at this time won't catch whoever is responsible."

Her forehead creasing in a frown, Mona leaned back against the seat. "You think it's a bigger operation?"

"Yeah. Who would have a tractor-trailer rig available to haul the cattle to market? Les and Wayne?" Reed shook his head.

The electronic tone of Mona's cell phone sounded over the truck's engine noise. She pulled it from her pocket. "Fernando?"

Reed slowed the vehicle, sliding over to the side of the road.

Mona's brows furrowed. "You sure they're not lost in the canyon?" Her gaze shot up to Reed's, her lips firming into a tight line. "Okay. Thanks for trying." She clicked the phone shut and stared ahead at the streets of Prairie Rock. "Not all the cattle escaped. Fernando and some of my uncle's ranch hands rounded up what they could find. Fifteen of the steers are still missing."

Reed shifted into drive and swung the truck back toward the center of town. He pulled into the county library and turned the key in the ignition, the engine noise stilled.

"Why are we here?" As she stared at the brick exterior of the tiny library, Mona's brows furrowed.

"We need access to the Internet." Reed climbed down from the truck and rounded to the passenger side. "We haven't looked at the locations of all the cattle since before the storm. Perhaps now we should."

Mona was already on the ground and headed for the library, her narrow hips twitching from side to side in the oversize shirt she wore.

Reed had never met a woman as stubbornly determined as Mona Grainger. As he trailed behind her into the cool interior of the small building, a smile tugged at the corners of his mouth.

Once inside, Mona sat at the computer. "Did you happen to bring the GPS numbers?"

He pulled a slip of paper from his pocket and handed it to her.

Within seconds, she had the tracking site up and the first cow located. As expected, it was situated somewhere on the property adjacent to Rancho Linda. The same story held true for the next four numbers. On the fifth, however, the computer zoomed in on a position far from the Rancho Linda. Closer to Amarillo.

"What do you want to bet that steer didn't walk all the way to Amarillo?"

Reed tapped her on the shoulder. "Let me." When she got up, he took the seat and narrowed their search to a street address. "Let's go see what we can find out about the delivery driver."

"I need to get back to the ranch before long. Fernando can't handle it all on his own, what with Jesse out of commission."

"A quick drive down to Amarillo and we'll head back to Rancho Linda to work that fence. Deal?"

"Absolutely. I want to nail whoever's behind the rustling so I can get on with what I do best."

Reed chuckled. "And what would that be?"

"Ranching." Her voice was stern, but when she turned away, a smile played with the corners of her luscious lips. Lips Reed hadn't been able to forget since the middle of last night's storm.

BY THE TIME they reached Amarillo, Mona was uncomfortable in more ways than one. On more than one occasion, she caught herself staring at Reed's hands, imagining them as they skimmed across her naked skin. The heat inside the air-conditioned truck had nothing to do with the outside temperature. She should have let Reed go by himself to Amarillo.

When the truck pulled to a stop in the gravel parking lot of the stockyard, Mona was out on the ground. "I'll meet you in the office area. I have to see a man about a horse."

Reed's brow wrinkled. "A horse? I thought—" His face reddened. "Oh, yeah. For the moment, I'd forgotten. I'll wait for you."

"No, go ahead and see what you can find out from the office personnel. I'll only be a minute." With the baby pushing against her bladder so hard she thought she'd wet her pants, she hurried to find the facilities.

As she entered the bathroom, she glanced back at the door to the office. Reed stepped through, looking confident and strong. Two things she wasn't feeling too much of lately. For the first time, the significance of her pregnancy hit her square in the gut. What would happen to her ranch when she couldn't ride out to check the fences and cattle? How could she manage? Tears welled in her eyes. She stepped into the stall and stood for a moment gulping in air, fighting back a wave of fear and self-doubt. She wasn't strong enough. She couldn't do it all.

The baby moved inside her, rolling from left to right. That little bit of movement brought her back to earth and to herself. No matter what happened, she had to look out for this life growing inside. The baby hadn't chosen its destiny, but she had and no matter what, this baby would know love and its heritage, like her father had shown her.

She completed her business and hurried out to find Reed exiting the sale-barn office followed by a rotund man in a dirt-stained blue shirt embroidered with Charlie's Auction over the left breast pocket.

The man had to be Charlie. He wore a straw cowboy hat and had a chaw of tobacco big enough to choke a horse lodged between his bottom row of teeth and his lip. "No, sir. We don't deal in stolen cattle here at Charlie's Auction. We have the newfan-gled chip readers and scan every steer and cow that comes through. Now, not all of them have microchips in 'em, mind you. Not all the ranchers can afford the luxury."

Mona joined them.

"Charlie Goodman, this is Mona Grainger, owner of the Rancho Linda." Reed stared hard at the man. "We have reason to believe some of the Rancho Linda cattle are in this sale barn without Ms. Grainger's permission. Some that are microchipped."

"We would have checked the registry when they were brought in. I'm sure you're mistaken."

"Then you won't mind if we have a look around using your chip reader, will you?"

"Not at all, as long as I don't have a shipment coming in. I'll even get my helper to assist." Charlie lifted a paper coffee cup and spit a dark stream of tobacco into it. "Just a minute while I find Gil." Charlie left them standing in the front entrance to the sale barn while he ducked through a door.

Mona stared after the man. "Do you trust him?"

"My instincts tell me he believes what he's saying."

"But the GPS said the cattle were here." Mona paced the short length of concrete flooring and back. "What if the GPS was wrong?"

"It was right." Reed stepped through the door Charlie had gone through, leaving Mona to stand there with her mouth open or follow.

She followed.

Charlie climbed down from the metal catwalk, a bead of sweat trickling down the side of his face.

"Don't know where Gil got to. I'll get the backup chip reader and be right back." He hurried past them, breathing hard.

When he returned with the device, he led them from pen to pen scanning several cattle from each lot and comparing them to the numbers Reed had in his pocket.

By the time they reached the last enclosure full of restless steers, Mona's spirits and energy were flagging. Had the GPS program been faulty?

Charlie ran his scanner over two animals in the last pen, neither of which indicated the presence of microchips. On the third steer, the device beeped and the numbers displayed, exactly matching one of the numbers Reed had with him.

Charlie's brows furrowed. "You say these numbers belong to the Rancho Linda?" He pulled a pen and pad from his pocket and jotted down the lot number. "Follow me."

Back in his office, he sat at a computer, the keyboard covered with a plastic protective shield, yellowed and stained with grease and dirt. He punched a few keys, bringing up a screen with the national registry of microchips. "Let me see those numbers you got there." He took the paper from Reed and keyed the numbers. "Ms. Mona Grainger," he read out loud. "Of the Rancho Linda. Care to show me your driver's license to make it all official?"

Mona dug in her purse and pulled out the license. "Can you tell me who brought the cattle in?"

He glanced at her license and looked up at her face. "Sure can." Pushing to his feet, he pulled a clipboard from the wall and flipped through several crinkled pages, stopping at the one with the same lot number on it as the one he'd jotted down on the pad. "Chase Molderhauer." He pointed at the printed name and the signature. The page also contained an address and phone number.

Mona pulled a pen and paper from her purse and wrote down the information.

"I don't have any idea how these cattle got past my crew here, but I can tell you, I don't cotton to cattle rustlin'. You have the word of Charlie Goodman on that." He looked down at the page, his lips tightening. "Gil Deiner was the man that checked that load of cattle in. I'll be havin' a word with him."

"Mind if I borrow your phone?" Reed asked.

"No, go right ahead."

As Mona watched, Reed dialed 911. "I'd like to report a crime." He paused. "Cattle rustling."

Mona felt a rush of relief. Finally, a real lead.

TWO HOURS LATER, a sworn statement by Reed, Mona and Charlie Goodman, and they were no closer to finding the man who'd deposited the cattle at the sale barn.

Reed finally took matters in his own hands. "If

you're done with us, we have work to do back at the ranch." He herded Mona out of the Amarillo police station and over to the truck.

She looked as if she'd blow over at the slightest gust of Texas wind. Once inside the truck, she sat silently staring forward. Even before they hit the road north to Prairie Rock, she'd slid sideways, her head resting against Reed's shoulder.

The woman didn't know when to cry uncle. She needed a long bubble bath and an even longer night's rest to recuperate.

Quietly, so as not to wake her, Reed pulled his cell phone from his pocket and dialed a friend who was with the Texas Department of Public Safety. "Hey, Jim, could you run a check on a Chase Molderhauer?"

His friend took the information, the sound of a keyboard clicking in the background. "You still with Sheriff Parker Lee out at Prairie Rock?"

Reed inhaled and let the breath out, weighing the consequences of lying or telling the truth. "No, I'm not."

"Glad to hear you're not with Parker Lee. He's a class-A jerk. Why don't you come on board with the DPS? We always have room for the good guys."

"Thanks, but I'm working for a pretty amazing outfit right now." He glanced down at Mona, whose head had found its way to his lap. Her breath warmed his thigh and her hand rested protectively against her belly. She was sound asleep. "If you could get me that information on Molderhauer, I'll owe you big-time."

"Not a problem. I'll do some digging and get right back to you."

"The sooner the better. And thanks, Jim."

As he flipped his phone shut, a movement from the right caught his attention. He slammed his foot on the brakes, but his reaction was too late.

A dark gray pickup burst out from behind a clump of mesquite and sagebrush, slamming into the right front fender of the Rancho Linda pickup.

The force of the blow spun the truck around and sent it careening across the road into the opposite ditch.

Mona screamed as the truck tilted sideways on two wheels before bouncing to a stop upright, the engine dying.

"Get down!" Reed grabbed her head and shoved her down. Shots rang out, pinging against the metal sides of the pickup, one shattering the driver's window.

The sound of tires squealing on blacktop was followed by a revving engine as the truck sped off to the north. Then silence filled the truck except for the sound of blood pounding against Reed's ears. "Mona? Are you okay?" He sat up and helped Mona sit straight as well.

"Yes, I think so." She pushed her hair out of her face, her eyes going wide. "You're bleeding." She reached up and touched his forehead, her fingers coming away with a bright red stain. "Let me take care of that." She tugged at the hem of her shirt, ripping a strip of cloth off the tail. When she pressed it to his forehead, her face came within inches of his, her brow creased and worried. "We shouldn't have come."

"Who would have guessed visiting a sale barn would illicit such a reaction? We couldn't have known."

"But you might have been killed." Her eyes filled. "All because of some stupid cows."

He grabbed her hand and held it in front of him. "The cattle aren't stupid. They're yours and no one has the right to steal them. It's my choice to work for you. If I didn't want to, I would walk away."

Her bottom lip trembled, her eyes liquid brown pools. "But I don't want you to die."

"I'm not going to." He kissed her fingertips. "Trust me."

She stared up into his face, one lonely tear trickling down her cheek. "It's so hard."

His chest constricted so tightly he thought he would have a heart attack. That one tear ripped at him until he leaned forward and kissed it away. "Quit worrying, boss lady, you were wrong about the cows."

"I was?"

"They're steers." He pulled her against him and kissed her, giving up on all his resolve to keep at a distance. How could he when she looked at him with frightened doe eyes?

Surprising him even more, she kissed him the way she had the night before when they'd lain in each other's arms with a storm raging around them. This woman had a truckload of worries on her shoulders and she worried about him. It was about time someone looked out for Mona Grainger.

He pushed her away and brushed the shattered glass from the seat. Then he shifted into park and twisted the key in the ignition. The engine turned over and died. Reed closed his eyes for a second, sending a prayer heavenward. Mona didn't need to walk home, not in her condition.

He opened his eyes and turned the key. The engine started, coughed and roared to full power.

Once on the road, Reed hurried back to Amarillo to report the incident to the sheriff's department. By the time they were back on the road to Rancho Linda, the sun had set and all the stars of the heavens shone down on them from a clear black sky.

Halfway back to Prairie Rock, Mona heaved a big sigh. "Do you think this nightmare will ever end?"

"Yes." Of that he was certain. He wasn't so sure about when or how.

The cell phone in his pocket vibrated against his chest before the ring tone sounded. "Reed here."

"It's Jim. Reed, I found something interesting about that name you asked me to check on."

"Shoot."

"I knew there was something familiar about the name Chase Molderhauer, just couldn't put my finger on it. So I ran a scan against known offenders."

"And?"

"Came up with nothing."

Disappointment knotted in Reed's gut. One more dead end. "Thanks for checking, Jim."

"Hey, wait up. I said he didn't show up in the known-offenders list, but the name rang a pretty big bell. I knew it from somewhere. So I did some digging and found a missing persons report for one Chase Molderhauer. The case was opened five months ago. As far as all the reports state, the man was never found. The family and state officials suspected foul play."

Chapter Fourteen

"That leaves us with more questions than answers, if you ask me." Mona stared at the truck parked in front of her house and moaned. Why did he have to show up when she had bigger problems to solve? "Is Molderhauer hiding from his family, having found cattle rustling more lucrative than sales? Or has someone assumed his identity to sell the stolen cattle without himself being fingered?"

"My friend said that Molderhauer's car was found with traces of blood on the steering wheel in Palo Duro Canyon. My bet would be whoever is rustling the cattle had something to do with Molderhauer's disappearance and possible death."

Mona dragged her feet through the front door of her house, tired to the bone and so dejected by the lack of definitive information she struggled to lift one foot after the other.

The last thing she needed was a confrontation from an estranged uncle paying her a visit so late at night.

"At last. I thought you'd never get here." Uncle Arty rose from the couch in her living room and strode toward her, looking so much like her father, Mona wanted to cry.

Sucking in a shaky breath, she squared her shoulders, prepared for battle. "What do you want? If you came to gloat, well, then get the hell out."

Her uncle stopped in midstride, his hat in his hands. His gaze raked over her from head to foot before he shook his head, a sad smile playing around his mouth. "I guess I deserved that." After a glance down at the black Stetson in his hands, he cleared his throat. "We have a problem."

Reed stepped up behind her and laid his hands on her tight shoulders, leaning her back against him. "Which one?"

"We found Dusty Gaither's body in the canyon close to where the cattle were taken. He'd been dumped behind a bush."

Blood rushed from Mona's head, leaving her dizzy. "How?"

Her uncle swallowed. "Shot in the back of his head."

Mona's knees buckled. If not for the support of the man behind her, she'd have dropped to the floor in a miserable heap.

Though she'd fired him the day before, she didn't wish ill on Dusty, even if he'd betrayed her. No one deserved death, especially a bullet to the back of his head.

Her uncle paced across the wood flooring of the living room and back. "I thought, at first, whoever killed him wanted it to look like I did it."

Mona shook her head, the room hazy in her sight. Reed eased her toward the couch, urging her to sit. When she did, her head didn't feel quite so fuzzy and she looked up at her uncle. "Why?"

"One of my guns was stolen from my gun cabinet. It was the same one used to kill Dusty. My fingerprints will be all over it because it's the one I used most recently shooting at rabbits. The gun was left beside the body. Pretty obvious, if you ask me." Her uncle shrugged. "I already reported it to the sheriff. I was surprised he didn't haul me in to jail. Maybe he's waiting for the state police to do the job."

"What the hell's going on?" When Mona leaned forward to push to her feet, a warm hand on her shoulder held her down.

Reed stood behind the couch, his hand firmly clamped on her. She wasn't going anywhere.

Too tired to argue, she sat back in the seat and spread her hands wide. "That's two men now. What's going on? Why won't this all stop?"

"What I'm more concerned about is that since they didn't take me in, they might look at other suspects. Since you've already been arrested on one murder charge and you were out all last night in the same location, they might come after you."

Mona closed her eyes and inhaled the lemony

scent of furniture polish, wishing she could keep her eyes closed and ignore her world imploding around her. "When did you find the body?"

"Fernando found him around sunset and called me immediately."

A stab of annoyance shot through Mona. Fernando had no reason to call her uncle. Any questions he had should have been directed to her. Then again, they might have been out of cell-phone range, the reception being spotty at best out in the wide-open spaces of the Texas panhandle.

Reed squeezed her shoulder and let go. "I'll be back in a minute." He gave her a stern look. "Stay put."

Mona glared at him, annoyance at his command and the entire situation making her testy. "I'll do as I please."

Her uncle plunked his hat on his head. "If you don't mind, I'm headed home. Be on the watch for Sheriff Lee. He's bound to come asking questions. I'm sorry this is all happening to you. You don't deserve it."

"Do I detect empathy?" Mona's brows rose. "Why the change of heart?"

Her uncle's feet shifted. "I never agreed with who your father married. That's no secret."

Mona opened her mouth to tell her uncle to get out, but he stopped her with his raised hand.

"After seeing how hard you've worked to keep this place afloat, I admit I was wrong. And since you're the only family I have left, I don't want to see you go under too. I'm sorry for all the grief I gave you and your father." He spun on his cowboy-booted heel and left.

Mona stared at the empty doorway, wishing her father was alive to witness his brother's about-face. Too bad he hadn't come to the same conclusion a year ago. Tom Grainger had never said a word about his brother, but Mona knew he grieved for the loss of the closeness they'd shared as children.

Mona wanted to crawl into the shower and then into bed to sleep until next week. Fat chance that would happen once Parker Lee sank his teeth into this murder. She'd probably end up accused of Dusty's demise as well. Mona had had her fill of law enforcement officials, false accusations and mug shots.

Reed returned to the living room, carrying a plate with a sandwich on it. "Your uncle left?"

"Yeah." Her stomach rumbling, Mona hadn't realized how long it had been since she'd eaten. The thought of facing another Parker Lee inquisition almost made her refuse the offering, but her baby had to have nourishment. She stood, accepted the plate and turned toward her bedroom. "I'll be in the shower. If anyone needs me, they'll have to drag me out in hand-cuffs." She hurried away before the dam burst.

Alone in her bedroom and even too tired to undress herself, Mona sat on the floor, biting into her sandwich. All of her troubles washed over her in endless waves until her eyes filled and her throat closed. She chewed, hoping eventually she could swallow again. Tears trickled down her cheeks, increasing in intensity until sobs shook her body. She dropped her sandwich on the plate and buried her face in her hands.

Too caught up in her misery to notice, she didn't realize someone else had entered the room until Reed sat on the floor beside her and gathered her in his arms. Wordlessly, he held her, stroking her back and pushing limp strands of her long black hair out of her wet face.

When her tears were spent, she leaned her cheek against his chest, the warmth of his body seeping into her cool skin, the special scent of leather and soap filling her senses.

She could get used to leaning on Reed Bryson. But how long would that last? Hadn't he said he would leave when her troubles were over?

With a work-roughened finger, he tipped her chin up. "All done?"

In more ways than one. Staring up into cool-green eyes, she could forget everything else around her. But another man had died and she was running out of suspects to question. "Yeah. I'm all done." She pushed against his chest and stumbled to her feet. "We have to get to Les and Wayne."

"You're not going tonight." He blocked her escape from the bedroom door. "You have to have sleep."

"I can't risk losing my last two sources of information."

"You have to rest."

Impatience surged inside. She planted her fists on her hips, prepared for battle.

Reed used a weapon even Mona couldn't resist. Guilt. "If you won't rest for yourself, do it for the baby." He reached out and touched the swell of her belly, the concern in his expression forcing her to consider his request.

As if responding to his voice, the baby kicked against his hand.

Mona gave in. "Okay, but first thing in the morning, we're going to have a talk with Les and Wayne."

"Agreed."

She just hoped they were still alive to answer questions. The way things were going, they'd be gone too. Then what?

REED LAY AWAKE half the night, listening for Mona, afraid she'd try to go see Les and Wayne by herself in the middle of the night.

She hadn't asked him to sleep with her and he hadn't pushed the issue. Their night in the cave might as well have been a dream to Mona.

Not to Reed. Every time he rolled over in the sheets, he wished he had her to roll up against, her body spooned against his, her dark hair spread across his pillow.

Around two o'clock in the morning he rose and took a cold shower to calm his galloping libido.

When sunrise finally graced the Texas skies, Reed didn't bother pretending to sleep anymore. He got up.

As he suspected, Mona was exhausted. She slept past her usual six o'clock. Not until eight did she rustle around in her bedroom, finally emerging wearing her signature jeans and baggy blue shirt.

How any woman could make the saggy, sloppy outfit look good, Reed didn't know. After thinking about her all through the long night, he just wanted to pull her into his arms as soon as he saw her. Instead, he handed her the plate of eggs and toast Rosa had prepared.

She pushed his offer away. "I don't have time to eat. I overslept and I want to get to Les and Wayne first thing."

He didn't give her a choice, he lifted her hand and set the plate in it. "Eat first, then we'll leave."

Mona sighed and sank into the chair proffered. "Where's Catalina?"

"Gone to work."

"To work? But she's barely out of the hospital."

"She insisted and actually, she looked all right. Plus, she wants to go in to Amarillo to check on Jesse when she gets off work." He smiled. "She said something about setting a few things straight."

Her head tipped to the side as Mona stared at Reed. "Did she say what she wanted to straighten out?"

He lifted his shoulders. "No. But she looked pretty determined."

"After we talk to Les and Wayne, we can swing by

Dee's." Before long, Mona had cleaned her plate, eating every last bite.

Reed smiled. "Where do you put it all? You're not any bigger than the dog I had growing up."

Mona rolled her eyes and stood, carrying her plate to the kitchen. "Oh please, don't overwhelm me with your compliments. That's the second time you've likened me to a dog. A girl can only take so much." When she returned from the kitchen, she wiped her hands on her jeans and said, "Okay, let's go."

The streets of Prairie Rock were busy at nine o'clock in the morning. Dee's Diner had cars parked around the block, the salty scent of bacon frying drifted through Reed's open truck window.

"Cat will be busy this morning. I hope she's up to it." Mona's soft smile turned into a hard, straight line as they drove past the diner and turned the corner to the body shop.

The two trucks parked out to the side of the shop yesterday weren't there this morning, and the place looked deserted.

Reed parked the truck around the side less visible from the road and climbed down. Mona followed. After a thorough search of the exterior, Reed dug a pocketknife from his jeans and jimmied the lock on the shop door. With only a little effort, he opened the lock and was stepping through.

Mona's gaze narrowed. "What did you say you did in Chicago?"

"I was a cop." He pushed the door inward and stepped out of the bright sunshine into the dingier office. "You coming?"

With a three-sixty glance darted around the street, Mona slipped in behind Reed. "Cop, huh? What are they training in cop school nowadays?"

"Whatever it takes." A smile lifted the corners of his lips as he entered the dark interior. After a quick scan of the papers scattered across Wayne's desk, Reed glanced up.

Mona had her hand clamped over her nose and mouth.

"Smell getting to you?"

She dropped her hand, her lips twisted. "How can you stand it? Last time I was here, it was all I could do not to throw up."

"I'm not pregnant." He carefully arranged the papers into their original disarray and moved toward the shop's bay area. "You want to wait outside in the truck?"

She straightened her shoulders. "No. Two pair of eyes have to be better than one."

Inside the shop, two vehicles were in various stages of repair. One was a black sport-utility vehicle, the front masked and taped with only the heavy-duty grille exposed, the paint chipped in one spot. The other was a silver economy car with the rear bumper removed.

Reed leaned into the open window of the sport-utility vehicle and spotted a blue light fixture, the kind used by unmarked police cars. He circled to the back of the vehicle for the license-plate number, but the plate had been removed.

Mona leaned into the passenger window and called out, "It's Parker Lee's unmarked car."

"How do you know it's his and not one of the other deputies'?"

"I dropped cherry soda on the floorboard a while back." She pointed inside. "The stain's still there."

Reed stared at her instead of the rug. "And why were you in the passenger seat?"

Mona walked to the front of the vehicle.

For a moment, Reed thought she wouldn't answer his question.

"I had a temporary lapse in sanity and dated the man." She stared across the hood of the truck at Reed. "What can I say? It was a mistake, I realized it and that's the end."

"Is Parker Lee your baby's father?"

Mona's gaze dropped to greasy concrete, her shoulders hunching. Then she pushed herself straight, her glance meeting his. "No one is going to take my baby away from me. Do you understand? Not Parker Lee or anyone else."

"You can't keep your pregnancy a secret, Mona. People are bound to talk. And when a baby shows up at the Rancho Linda, someone's bound to do the math."

"I can't let him take my baby from me."

"Why would he?"

"You know Parker Lee. He's a small-minded,

mean man. I just didn't see it soon enough. If he knew I was pregnant with his child, he'd take my baby, my ranch and everything I own." She waded through the tools and parts to Wayne's office. "I won't let that happen."

"Unfortunately, the legal system thinks a father has the right to know."

"To hell with the legal system!" She spun to face him, her eyes rounded. "You aren't going to tell him, are you?"

Reed shook his head. "Your secret's safe with me."

"Good." She inhaled and let the air out slowly. "If there's nothing to find here, let's go by the diner and see if Les and Wayne are having breakfast."

He crossed in front of her and blocked her from stepping out into the Texas sunshine. "Really, Mona, you can't keep the secret for much longer." He touched a hand to her belly. "Your condition is becoming more evident by the day."

She pushed around him and out the door. Her bottom lip trembled and was that a tear leaking from the corner of her eye? "Don't bother worrying about me. I've managed on my own since my father died. I can continue."

Reed locked Wayne's office and hurried to catch up with Mona. "Maybe, but you'll get to the point you can't do it all by yourself. Then what?"

"Then I'll hire another ranch hand." She beat him to the driver's side and climbed behind the wheel.

When he got in the passenger seat, she held out her hand. "Keys."

His brows drew together but, rather than argue, he handed her the truck keys. At least now he knew for certain Parker Lee was the father. And she was right, the man was mean. If he thought someone was pulling a fast one on him, he'd go for the throat. No wonder she'd kept that information close to her chest.

She drove the short blocks to Dee's Diner. The crowd was beginning to thin, but there were still a healthy number of cars parked around the eatery.

Mona didn't wait for Reed to open her door. She was opening the door to the diner by the time he reached her.

"Mona!" Catalina hurried across the smoothly polished black-and-white tile floor, the usual coffee carafe in one hand.

"Hi, Cat. How are you feeling?" Mona stared at her friend, touching a hand to the bruise on her cheekbone.

Catalina smiled. "Besides a residual headache and a couple of bruised ribs, I'm okay and I'm glad I came in. We had a lot of customers and Kelly called in sick. Let me find you a table." She glanced around the busy room, spotted a table in the far corner and pointed to it with the carafe. "Take that one. I'll have the busboy clean it up."

Mona and Reed eased between empty tables littered with dirty dishes and napkins. When they reached the table Catalina had indicated, Mona dropped into the chair facing the door.

Reed sat beside her, not across from her, so that he'd have a similar view.

Mona groaned and dropped her face in her hands.

"What's wrong?" Reed placed a hand to her forehead. "Are you sick?"

"Yeah. Jeffrey Kuhn just came in."

Reed recognized the man as the president of Prairie Creek's one and only bank. He strode in dressed in a suit and shiny leather shoes, his attire standing out among the typical blue jeans and cowboy boots. "So?"

"Look, you might as well know—" Mona took a deep breath "—he's threatening foreclosure on Rancho Linda if I don't pay the note in full by the end of the month."

"Why?"

"I've been so busy working the ranch, I didn't look at all the bills like I should have. Dad had a balloon note due this year."

"Won't the bank refinance?"

Mona's lips thinned. "Kuhn said that the bank has lost faith in my ability to meet my obligations and feels it's prudent for me to find other means to finance my loan or sell my property."

Kuhn glanced her way, eyes narrowing. His gaze raked over Reed before he found a table as far away from Mona as he could get.

Coward. Reed started to stand, ready to put his fist through the man's teeth for giving Mona hell.

Mona grabbed his arm and shook her head. "He's not worth it. I'll find a way to manage. Don't worry. I've never missed payroll with my employees."

"I could care less about payroll, the man has no right to put that kind of burden on you."

"Well, apparently he does." She shrugged. "I've got loan applications out to several banks in Amarillo, but they tell me my credit rating is in the toilet."

"Have you ever missed payments?"

"Never. And my father was a stickler for making payments on time."

"Sounds like someone's jerking you around." If not for Mona's hand, Reed would have stalked across the diner and demanded answers from the banker.

"I'll figure it out. But first, we need to find Wayne and Les. One problem at a time. My cattle come first."

"You won't have to worry about your cattle if you lose the ranch."

The corners of her mouth turned downward. "I refuse to believe that will happen."

Catalina wove her way through the tables with a big plastic tub balanced on one hip. "We're down one busboy as well as Kelly. Must be something going around." She cleaned up the dishes and wiped the table. "I guess you heard about Dusty? Papa told me last night."

Mona nodded. "Yeah."

Reed and Mona helped Catalina place dishes and cups in the tub.

"I don't like to speak ill of the dead," Catalina said, "but I have a feeling he had it coming to him. Working for you, dipping in your uncle's pocket and probably knee deep in the cattle rustling as well."

"That's why we're here." Mona placed the last glass on top of the rest of the dishes. "I think Dusty is dead because he knew too much about the rustling. Cat, have you seen Les and Wayne this morning?"

"No. But someone mentioned they'd gone to Oklahoma to one of the casinos last night. Maybe they didn't make it back. Why? Do you think they're involved as well?"

"We don't know. But they might have some answers." Mona's gaze shot to the door. "Great. Just when I thought the day couldn't get worse."

The Teague Oil & Gas men held the door open and a woman stepped into the diner, looking as if she was walking into a fancy restaurant in New York City. She wore a tailored navy blue suit that fit her slim body to perfection and complemented her pale complexion. Although she walked as if she owned the place, dark circles shone through the carefully applied concealer, and her eyes darted from person to person inside the diner. When she spotted Kuhn, her brows arrowed downward and she turned around in the doorway.

The two Teague speculators blocked her way. When they moved to let her pass through to the street, she hesitated, her hands fluttering. Instead of leaving, she straightened and made her way to a table in the middle of the diner, her head held high. She sat with her back to the door, casting sideways glances at Kuhn.

Mona eyed the group as if waiting for them to converge on her and talk her into selling. She recognized the two men, but not the woman. "Who is she?" she asked.

Catalina snorted softly. "You recognize the guys as the speculators who work for Teague Oil & Gas. Well, meet Teague."

"She's Teague?"

"Patricia Teague, widow of Andrew Teague. She comes to town once in a while, I guess to check on her investments."

"What's she doing in the diner?"

"I don't know." Catalina shifted a few plates and glasses in the tub. "But the way things have been this morning, you'd think this place was Grand Central Station. Did you hear about the guy who got run off the road last night?"

Mona shook her head. "No."

"Some guy from Amarillo wrecked just outside Prairie Rock. His truck was flipped, killing him instantly."

"That's too bad."

"Yeah, half the deputies in the county were in here earlier after cleaning up the accident scene. They said there were black paint marks on the back of the bumper. They think he was forced off the road. A hit-and-run. That and Dusty's death have been the talk of the morning."

Mona's face grew serious. "Do they know who it was? Anyone we know?"

"Not anyone I know." Catalina tipped her head to the left and stared at the ceiling. "Someone named Dilbert or Gilbert Dean, I think. Something like that."

Reed's heartbeat sped up. "Could it have been Gil Deiner?"

"That's the name." Catalina lifted the tub onto her hip. "Look at me gossiping. Let me dump this stuff and grab a headache pill. I'll be right back for your order."

"No hurry, Cat." Mona waited until Cat moved away before whispering, "Another witness gone. We have to find Les and Wayne."

Reed agreed with Mona. He was leaning forward to stand and suggest they drive around town looking for the two, when another thought occurred to him. He sat back in his seat. "What if they were the ones who forced Gil off the road?" He didn't want Mona anywhere near the two men in that case.

The diner door opened and Grace Bryson walked in, her steps slow and labored. She turned to thank her husband for holding the door, giving him the lopsided smile of one recovering from a stroke. Despite the distortion, the soft look of love for her husband was evident in her eyes. She looked almost as young and beautiful as the picture of her and

William on their wedding day. The wrinkles around her eyes and mouth only accentuated her maturity.

To Reed, she'd always been the most beautiful mother a kid could have.

And the care with which William Bryson cupped her elbow and helped her along went against everything Reed knew about his stepfather. When had the man ever shown his wife any kind of love? He'd seemed angry at her and everyone else in the world ever since Reed could remember. Had his mother's illness changed him? Or was it that he no longer had a ranch to deal with, which gave him the time to dedicate to the woman he'd sworn to love, honor and cherish?

Whatever it was, Reed found his anger toward his stepfather fading. Knowing that his mother would be loved and taken care of made all the difference. The entire reason he'd come back to Prairie Rock in the first place was to make sure she had the care she needed. He hadn't trusted his stepfather to do it. And William Bryson had proven him wrong.

"Reed?" Mona rested her hand on his arm, her touch light and questioning. "Who are they?"

"My parents." He pushed to his feet and walked across the floor. "Mom, Mr. Bryson, I'd like you to meet someone."

His mother frowned at the formal way he addressed his stepfather, but she didn't say anything. Instead, she leaned against her husband and started toward Mona, sitting at the back of the room.

They didn't get more than two tables deep into the diner, when a keening wail rent the air. Patricia Teague stood up so fast her chair tipped backward and crashed to the floor. She stared at Reed's mother, her face fading to a sickly green. Then a hot flush of red filled her pale cheeks and she rushed across the floor, pushing chairs aside, her fingers curled into claws. "You! You home wrecker!" She lunged at Reed's mother. "Bitch!"

William Bryson curled his wife into his arms and Reed stepped between the crazed woman and his mother.

She hit Reed full in the chest with the power of her assault, her shoulder crashing against his ribs.

Reed grunted under the force of the woman's body, but held steady. "It's all her fault! Jezebel!" She raised her fingernails to Reed's face. Sinking one in before he could ward her off. "Get out of my way! Let me at her."

Reed grabbed her wrists, holding away from his face her sharp-tipped fingernails, stained in subtle pink nail polish and the dark red of his blood.

He turned, with the woman still in his grip, and stared at his mother. "Mother, do you know this woman?"

His mother stared back at Patricia Teague and nodded, tears springing to her eyes. "Yes, I do," she said in blurred words.

"She should, she ruined my marriage the night before my wedding. She's a snake! Don't trust her." The woman struggled, kicking her pointy-toed shoes.

The woman who, a moment before, had been the epitome of grace and style now spewed venom with every word she spoke. Her carefully coiffed hair shook loose of the pins and fell over eyes quickly filling with tears. "You ruined my life." She sagged into Reed, tears leaving a trail of mascara down her cheeks.

"I'm sorry for what happened," his mother said, reaching out for the woman. "But it wasn't my fault."

Patricia Teague pulled herself away from Reed. "The hell it wasn't." For the first time, she stared up at the man still holding her wrists and her face went ghostly white. She stared from Reed, over her shoulder to Jeffrey Kuhn and back. Then passed out in Reed's arms.

Chapter Fifteen

When Patricia Teague had flung herself at Reed, Mona came out of her chair and raced across the diner, every protective instinct she had inside hurrying to Reed's aid.

Not that Reed Bryson needed help. A thin, delicate woman like Patricia Teague was no match for Reed's hard-earned muscles.

The crazed woman got in only one swipe of her claws across his cheek before he subdued her.

Blood oozed from the cuts, dripping in long red streaks down his jaw. Mona was reaching for Reed's face with clean napkins when Patricia Teague passed out. She'd been staring into Reed's face and then looked over at Jeffrey Kuhn. What had she seen that made her turn as white as a newborn sheep?

Mona's gaze went from one man to the other, a chill creeping across her skin.

Every bit as tall as Reed, Jeffrey Kuhn wasn't nearly as filled out in the shoulders. Both men had green eyes. Although Kuhn had graying blond hair, he also had a square jawline, just like Reed.

If she wasn't mistaken, the two men shared a bloodline. A pretty darned close one at that.

"Someone call 911," Reed called, stretching Patricia out on the floor.

Dee Stacker emerged from the kitchen carrying a worn army blanket and a dusty pillow. She handed the items to Mona, who stood closest to Reed and Patricia.

Mona draped the blanket over the woman and the pillow beneath her head.

"Did you see that?" Catalina nodded toward the door. Jeffrey Kuhn had just left the diner.

"He didn't even pay his bill." She planted her fists on her hips. "That's okay. I'll get him next time he comes in."

Prairie Rock's volunteer Emergency Medical Services, only a block away, arrived minutes after Patricia fell into Reed's arms. The crowd moved outside the diner to give the emergency personnel room to work.

The sheriff's squad car spun around the corner and skidded to a halt. Sheriff Parker Lee leaped from the car and strode over to where Reed and Mona stood. "What's going on?"

"Mrs. Teague went crazy and passed out," Mona said.

The EMS technicians wheeled the gurney carrying

Patricia Teague out of the diner and toward the back of the ambulance.

The sheriff got back in his car and led the ambulance away from the diner, lights flashing.

Grace Bryson laid a hand on Reed's arm. "We need to talk. Would you come back to the house with me?"

"Of course." He turned to Mona. "Stay here. I'll be back in a few minutes and we'll find Wayne and Les." Reed's face was set in a mask as he led his mother away from the diner, his father following behind.

Mona shook her head. "What the heck just happened?"

"I don't know, but my guess is there's a history between Patricia Teague and Grace Bryson." Catalina stared after Reed and his family. "I'd give my eyeteeth to be a fly on the wall in the conversation she's fixin' to have with your man Reed."

"He's not my man," Mona said absently, her mind struggling to wrap itself around what Patricia said before she passed out. Grace Bryson had ruined her marriage? "I just wonder how Grace Bryson ruined Patricia Teague's marriage." Since she hadn't been invited to the show-and-tell with Reed's parents to get her answers, Mona decided to take the matter into her own hands.

"When Reed comes back, tell him I'll be at the library."

Catalina frowned. "I thought he told you to stay put."

Mona smiled at her friend. "How much danger can I get into at the library?"

"Knowing you, a lot." Catalina shook her head. "But my telling you not to go won't do any good, will it?"

Mona shook her head.

"That's what I thought." Catalina sighed. "Be careful out there. With three people dead, the odds aren't looking good for the citizens of Prairie Rock."

"If it makes you feel better, I'll take the truck."

"It does." Catalina stood in the doorway to the diner, rubbing the back of her head, a reminder that whoever was playing this game played rough.

The library was only two blocks away. Reed could walk that more easily than she could. Though she'd lived near Prairie Rock all her life and gone to school in the town, she couldn't help looking over her shoulder as she climbed down from the truck. Even in broad daylight, she didn't feel safe. The street was deserted, most of the activity still back at the diner.

Once inside, she pulled up a chair in front of the computer and checked in the newspaper archives for any references to Patricia Teague and Grace Bryson.

Her efforts were rewarded with a plethora of newspaper articles about the wealthy widow of Andrew Teague.

Mona scanned article after article going all the way back to the Austin society column announcing Andrew Teague's engagement to a relatively unknown woman, Patricia Lee Kuhn.

Within four years of his marriage, Andrew died of a heart attack, leaving Patricia the wealthiest widow in the state of Texas.

Patricia Kuhn. Had Patricia been married to Jeffrey Kuhn before Teague? Mona performed a search on Patricia Kuhn and found a wedding announcement for Jeffrey Kuhn and Patricia Lee Taylor, dating back thirty-two years.

Mona guessed the Kuhn marriage was the one Patricia had referenced when she'd accused Grace of ruining it for her. What had Mrs. Bryson done to ruin that marriage? And did Reed know anything about it? She'd bet he'd know after his little talk with his parents.

There were only three articles on Grace Bryson. One dated back thirty-two years to her wedding announcement to William Bryson. A month after the Kuhn wedding. The second article was eight months later with the birth announcement of Reed Charles Bryson. The third, most recent article involved the sale of the Bryson ranch to L & T Oil after Grace's stroke.

The ranch had fallen on hard times following a drought-induced prairie fire that killed seventy-five percent of their herd. Mona remembered that fire. The Rancho Linda had to reposition their herd just in case the winds shifted and sent the flames back toward their property.

With no connection to be found between Patricia and Grace, Mona ran a scan on Teague Oil & Gas. The articles dated over twenty years. The most recent information dealt with purchases made in the panhandle around Prairie Rock. In one article both Lang Oil Exploration and Teague Oil & Gas had been locked in a bidding war for one particular property. Teague, with their vast cash reserves, won out.

"Need help?" Ann Gooding, the librarian, looked over Mona's shoulder. "Trying to decide which oil company to sell to? I'd go with Teague. I hear Lang is on the verge of filing for bankruptcy if they don't find a new well soon."

"How do you know?"

"Let me." Ann took control of the computer mouse and clicked a view of that morning's news release from a Dallas newspaper. "Lang's been beat out by Teague in just about every deal over the past six months. And the land and mineral rights they've purchased haven't panned out. Whoever's feeding them information should be fired." Ann stepped back, leaving the mouse to Mona. "I pity the investors."

"You're telling me." Then why had Jeffrey Kuhn pushed Lang Oil Exploration as a potential purchaser for the Rancho Linda? Her breath caught in her throat. Kuhn had to be one of the duped investors.

Maybe it was time she asked what was in it for him. "Thanks for the information." Mona logged off and left, headed for the bank. She felt frivolous driving when she could just as easily have walked the two blocks.

Inside, she smiled at the teller she recognized as Nora Cleary. "Is Mr. Kuhn in his office?"

"I haven't seen him since he left over an hour ago, but I've been on break. Let me check." She left her position and walked down the back hallway to Mr. Kuhn's office. After a short knock, she waited a sufficient amount of time, and then opened the door. "Mr. Kuhn, Ms. Grainger would like to speak to you."

Mona pushed past the clerk and entered the office. "Thank you, Miss Cleary." Nora backed out of the office and closed the door behind her.

"I'm sorry, Miss Grainger, I don't have time to talk with you."

"Perhaps you should make time." Mona stalked up to his desk and leaned her hands on it, getting as close to the man in the leather seat as possible. "I don't know what all that was about back there at the diner, but I did some digging and found out some interesting facts. Would you like me to tell you what I learned?"

"No, actually, I'm late for an appointment." He rose.

"Sit down, Mr. Kuhn." Mona didn't shout, but she leveled a killer look at the man who'd made her life miserable over the last few days.

He hesitated, then sat.

"I found that the oil company you've been pushing me to sell to is filing for bankruptcy." Her brows rose. "Why would a banker suggest I sell my ranch to a business about to go under?"

"I had no idea they weren't solvent." He shuffled

the papers on his desk without meeting her eyes. "What exactly are you trying to imply?"

Mona's brows rose farther. "Tell me, Mr. Kuhn, do you or your bank have investments in Lang Oil Exploration?"

He blanched, his hands curling around the knife-like letter opener lying on his desk. "I don't think that's relevant. Now, if you'll excuse me."

"I'm right, aren't I? Either you or the bank are investors in the Lang holdings."

Kuhn leaned forward, his green eyes blazing. "And they would have made a lot of money with the purchase of Rancho Linda."

"Only problem is that I'm not selling." Mona backed away. "Put a little dent in your plans?"

"You will sell. You can't afford that place. Not with the loss of your cattle."

"I suppose that's your doing, isn't it?"

"Oh no. I'm not the one responsible for that. I don't know who is, but whoever it is couldn't have timed it better." This time Jeffrey Kuhn walked around the desk to stand face-to-face with Mona.

"You're Reed's real father, aren't you?"

His green eyes narrowed. "Again, I don't know what you're talking about. If you don't leave my office now, I'll be forced to call the sheriff."

"I can see the resemblance." He was as tall as Reed and their eyes the same color. "You had an affair with his mother before you married Patricia, didn't you?"

He picked up the telephone. "I'm calling the sheriff."

"Go ahead. I'll tell him you're behind the rustling. That you've embezzled the bank's money to invest in speculative oil exploration." She planted her fists on her hips. "Go ahead, call the sheriff."

"You have no proof."

"I won't need any. You'll be so tied up in court, whatever money you've sunk into Lang will be long gone by the time they clear up the mess." Mona pulled her cell phone from her back pocket and flipped it open. "What's the number? Ah yes…911."

A muscle in Kuhn's jaw flickered and a red stain rose up in his cheeks. He snatched the letter opener from the desk, grabbed Mona's hair and yanked her head back. With the tip of the letter opener to her throat, he growled a warning. "You won't call the sheriff."

"Too late. I already did." She held her phone up for him to see it make the connection.

Kuhn slapped the phone from her hand and flung her against his desk.

Pain seared through her hip.

"You stupid bitch." He paced away from her, running his fingers through his hair while he rolled the letter opener in the palm of his other hand. "This wouldn't have happened if you'd just sold the ranch when your father passed. None of it!" He stopped and glared at her. "You should have sold."

"I don't sell out on my family."

He marched across the floor and grabbed her shirt,

holding her up until her feet dangled and she couldn't breathe. "What's that supposed to mean?" He stared into her face. "I didn't divorce Patricia, she divorced me and took away my son. She was the one who left me." He dropped his hold and stepped back, staring at his hands.

Mona gulped in a breath of air. "After you cheated on her?"

"We weren't even married then."

A knock sounded on the door and Nora Cleary stuck her head inside. "A couple deputies are in the lobby insisting on seeing you. What do you want me to tell them?"

Jeffrey Kuhn glared at Mona before he answered in an unsteady tone, "I'll be right out."

Miss Cleary closed the door.

"Go on." Kuhn jerked his head toward the door.

"I'll leave when you leave. I don't trust you not to sneak out."

"There are no windows that open in my office and you can wait outside the door if it makes you feel better. Is it too much to ask for a moment alone to call my lawyer?"

Mona's eyes narrowed, but she'd gotten what she wanted. "You bet on the wrong horse, Mr. Kuhn. That land will remain in my family until I die."

He stared up at her from his leather chair, his gaze vacant. "That might be sooner than you think."

"Is that a threat?"

"Not from me. But there are other, less scrupulous people who would kill to get their hands on that land."

"Who?"

"You think you have everything figured out…*you* guess. Now get out."

The hard set to his chin convinced Mona she'd have more success pulling teeth from a Brahman bull. She'd be better off telling what she knew to the deputies. Mona left, closing the door behind her as Jeffrey Kuhn lifted the telephone.

She waited in the hallway outside his office to make sure he didn't make a run for the back door. Not that she could do much to stop the big man. Her throat still hurt from his iron grip. But at least she could tell the cops which direction he went.

As she entered the lobby and spotted Deputy Phillips, a loud bang rattled the windows.

Instinct forced her to drop to the ground.

An alarm went off inside the bank and the deputies charged through the hall doorway.

Deputy Phillips bent down and touched her on the back. "Miss Grainger, are you all right?"

"I'm fine."

"Can you move?" he asked.

"Yes, of course." Her knees were shaking so badly, she didn't really know if she could stand, but she made the effort.

The other deputy cupped her elbow and hurried

her away from the doorway and out into the lobby. "Evacuate the bank. Now!"

Mona didn't have to be told twice. She ran for the door and out into the hot light of day. Nora and the other clerk were the only employees in the lobby, and they stood outside on the sidewalk with Mona. "What do you suppose happened?" Nora asked, wringing her hands together. "Why hasn't Mr. Kuhn come out yet?"

Deputy Phillips walked out of the bank, followed by his partner. He pulled the radio from his belt and pressed the side. "We need an ambulance at the Prairie Rock Bank. Got an apparent suicide. One man down, no other casualties."

Mona leaned against the side of the building, fighting off a wave of nausea.

While Deputy Phillips asked her questions and wrote down her statement, an ambulance arrived. The same one that had taken Patricia Teague earlier. Had it really been over an hour since that incident? Mona stared at the bank's digital sign, blinking ninety-four degrees and eleven o'clock, the message repeating every twenty seconds.

Was that it? Another man dead, a woman on her way to the nuthouse and Mona still didn't know who'd been rustling her cattle or killing people right and left. Where was Reed? "Are you through with me?" she asked Deputy Phillips.

"Just a minute more. Sheriff Lee wanted to have

a word with you about Mr. Kuhn. He'll be here in a few minutes."

Her stomach rumbled, reminding her it was lunch-time. Not that she felt like eating, but if she didn't, she'd get dizzy and nausea would surely follow. Shouldn't Reed be back by now? "Damn." She'd told Catalina that she'd be at the library. "Can you tell the sheriff I'll be at the diner?"

"I suppose. But don't go too far. He insisted he wanted to question you himself."

"Fine." Not that she'd have anything different to say. If he wanted to talk to her, he could come find her.

When Mona left the bank, she was still shaking. But she decided to swing by the body shop to see if Wayne and Les had ever shown up. She didn't plan on stopping. Not without her backup, Reed. But at least she could tell him whether or not they were there and she could come back when she had more support with her. As she rounded the street corner, Wayne's one-ton pickup, hauling a trailer loaded with three four-wheelers on the back, spun out of the gravel parking lot headed out of town.

"Damn!" Mona's foot hesitated between brakes and the accelerator. She couldn't let them get away, but she couldn't go it alone. Reed had to know where she was going and why.

She fumbled in her pocket for her cell phone, dropping it on the floorboard on the opposite side of the truck. "Double damn!"

Lifting her foot from the accelerator, she reached as far as she could, but the phone was out of reach. She'd have to park to get to it. In the meantime, Wayne and Les had pulled way ahead of her on the highway leading out of Prairie Rock and toward Palo Duro Canyon.

Should she stop and lose sight of the two? Or follow them long enough to get an idea of where they were going? After all the trouble these two had caused, she'd be damned if she let them go now. But she'd be stupid not to call.

Two miles out of town, Mona pulled to a stop in the middle of the empty road and crawled across the seat to the cell phone. Unfortunately, when she flipped it open, she had only minimal reception. Probably not enough for a call. She dialed Reed's number anyway, hoping she could at least get a message to him.

She almost jumped with joy when it rang, her joy evaporating when the phone went immediately to his voice mail. The static in her ear didn't bode well for leaving a message. She tried anyway. "Reed, I'm on the highway headed toward Palo Duro Can—" A siren sounded behind her, making her jump.

Sheriff Parker Lee stepped out of his unmarked black sports-utility vehicle and ambled her way. Good, maybe he could help.

She hurriedly added to her message, "Les and Wayne are in front of me with the four-wheelers.

The sheriff's pulled up behind me, but get here soon!" Well before her words ran out, the static disappeared and the call died. How much of the message he could decipher, she didn't know. A quick glance at the phone confirmed all reception was lost.

"Mona, Mona, Mona." The sheriff opened her truck door, a smile tilting his lips. "What are you doing way out here by yourself?"

Mona practically fell out of the truck. For the first time since their disastrous lovemaking, she was happy to see the man. "Parker, you have to stop them." She pointed toward the disappearing truck and trailer.

"Who?" He grabbed her arms and held her still. "Who do I have to stop, Mona?"

"Les and Wayne. I saw them with a trailerload of muddy four-wheelers. They have to be the ones who were in on the cattle rustling. Hurry, or they'll get away!"

"I'll take care of it. Come on, you can ride with me." He shut her truck door and led her to his vehicle, opening the back door to let her climb in. "I'd let you ride up front, but with all the new computer equipment, there's just not room."

Not until Mona climbed in and the door was shut did she get her first inkling that something wasn't right. Starting with the sport-utility vehicle. She'd seen it over an hour ago in Les and Wayne's body shop covered with tape and drop cloth. But all the tape had been removed and the grille's paint was dry. "Did you have this car in the shop for repairs?"

"As a matter of fact, I did."

To the grille. The *black* grille. Didn't Catalina say that Gil Deiner's car had been run off the road by a vehicle that left black paint on the bumper? A cold chill slithered down her spine and the baby slammed a heel into her rib cage.

"That Les and Wayne do good, fast work when they have a little incentive."

She was afraid to ask but couldn't stop herself. "Incentive?"

"Yeah, incentive." Sheriff Lee glanced at her in the mirror, his brown eyes almost black, like a devil's fathomless pit. "Yeah. Let's hope your boyfriend figures it all out fast, or you'll die. I call that incentive."

Chapter Sixteen

"Patricia Teague was partially right. Because of me, her marriage never lasted." Sitting across the kitchen table in her little cottage on the edge of Prairie Rock, Reed's mother looked as pale and fragile as when she'd been released from the hospital following her stroke.

"It wasn't your fault." William placed his hand over hers. "Had I known what happened at the time, things would have been a lot different."

She squeezed his fingers, her gaze never leaving Reed's face. "I worked with Jeffrey Kuhn as a clerk in the bank. He was a young loan officer. On the night before his wedding, he said he was having second thoughts and was really scared about it." Grace Bryson looked away from her son, her gaze staring off into the distance as if she was looking back all those years. "He said he needed someone to talk with to help him over his prewedding jitters." She laughed a mirthless laugh. "I offered to listen and help if I could, in return he said he'd take me home. My parents were older and lived a couple miles out of town. I didn't see anything wrong with it, and Jeffrey had never led me to believe he'd do something stupid. He knew I was engaged to your father. We were due to marry in a month, which was why I was so receptive to his request. So we talked for an hour over coffee at the diner."

His mother's hands gripped William's. "When he drove me out to my parents', he passed the turnoff and kept going out toward Palo Duro Canyon, to an old hunting lodge he and his family used during hunting season."

"The one the teens used to smoke marijuana in?" Reed asked.

"Yes, that's the one. Nothing good ever happened in that cabin. When I insisted he take me home, he laughed and dragged me inside and…and…" Tears welled in her eyes.

Reed's chest hurt, his own throat choking on his mother's pain. "Mom, you don't have to go on."

She looked across at him and through her tears said in a strong, determined voice, "Yes, I do. You need to understand. It wasn't my choice. I didn't make love to Jeffrey Kuhn. He raped me."

"Why didn't you turn him in to the police?"

"He held a pretty big weapon. One I didn't see any way around at the time. As the loan officer at the only bank in town, he held the loan on William's land. He said that if I told the police, he'd make sure the loan foreclosed and William would lose everything.

"The land had been in William's family for a century. I couldn't let him lose it. Jeffrey married Patricia Lee Taylor the next day in a big, fancy wedding. Who would believe me, if I told the police I'd been raped by one of the rising stars of Prairie Rock the night before his wedding?

"The rape would have to remain a secret. I lied to my parents, I lied to William and I lied to you to keep from losing the land." She stared into her husband's eyes. "My lies caused you both so much pain. William hated me because he thought I cheated on him. He hated you because you were another man's son, not his, but he never told another soul."

"Because I was ashamed." William cupped Grace's palm to his cheek. "I thought I was your second choice, that you only married me because you had to."

"Never." She smiled, her pretty, gray-blue eyes glassy with tears. "I've always loved you."

"I don't know how. I was angry for so long, I could have lost you. You should have divorced me long ago." He pressed a kiss into her hand.

"No, I couldn't. I loved you then, I love you now."

Everything they said to each other played out like a movie. Reed felt as though he was intruding. And Mona wouldn't stay put long. "I should go."

"No, don't." The man Reed had thought was his

father all those years looked to him now, sorrow etched into the deep, tanned lines around his eyes. "I couldn't look at you without seeing what I thought was her betrayal. I was wrong. So wrong." William Bryson, who'd pretended to be his father for all those years, the stoic, hard man who'd never so much as smiled, cried silent tears. He scrubbed his face with the back of his sleeve. "You did nothing to deserve my temper. You were just a kid. A good one at that. I'm sorry."

A few days ago, Reed wouldn't have been as forgiving or as easily assuaged. But having met Mona and witnessed how determined she was to retain what was hers and protect the ones she loved, he could well understand what his mother had done and even how his stepfather had behaved. "Why tell the secret now?"

"I couldn't tell the secret or William would have lost his ranch. After a while, it just didn't matter. The time went by and I just let it go."

"Until Grace had her stroke and I sold the ranch." William clutched Grace's hand in his. "I thought I'd lost her."

"I wanted William to know the truth about you and you to know what happened."

"Why did Patricia blame you for her failed marriage?" Reed asked.

"She knew. I don't know how, but she knew. Maybe Jeffrey told her. Maybe she saw us at the diner together. But she knew. It must have eaten at her. She had a baby within nine months after their wedding. A boy, Jeff Jr. He'd be about the same age as you. He looked more like her, dark hair, dark eyes, whereas you looked like Jeffrey. A reminder that he'd had me first." Grace's lips twisted. "They argued bitterly, dragging it into the public. She'd call Jeffrey names in front of the boy. Finally, she filed for divorce and left with Jeff Jr. I heard she changed their names and disappeared for a while. Then she started showing up here six years ago with Teague Oil & Gas."

"Whatever happened to her son?" Reed asked.

"I don't know." Grace sighed. "I need to rest. All this excitement…"

Reed stood and helped his mother to her feet.

William hooked his hand through her arm. "I'll take care of her. You go back to your girl. She needs you now."

When Reed turned to leave, his mother's voice stopped him.

"Reed?" Grace stood in the curve of her husband's arm. "I hope you can forgive us."

Seeing the two of them holding on to each other made his heart ache with the need to find a love as strong. One woman came to mind and she was waiting back at the diner for him. "It would be a waste of time if I didn't."

"Do you need a ride back to the diner?" William asked.

"No, I'll walk. It's not that far." The mile would give him time to digest everything they'd told him. As he strode along the street, passing wood-framed houses dating back to the early fifties and some newer brick homes, he mulled over what had happened.

That snake, Jeffrey Kuhn, the man who'd threatened to foreclose on Mona's property was the same man who'd raped Reed's mother over thirty years ago. His father. By blood only. The man could never be a good father, he didn't have it in him. Rage burned inside Reed and he wanted to pummel the man into a bloody heap.

The sound of sirens wailed ahead of him, jerking him out of his rage. What now?

Mona? His footsteps increased until he was running on the pavement, wishing he'd worn tennis shoes rather than cowboy boots. When he turned the corner onto Main Street, an ambulance pulled away from the front of the Prairie Rock Bank. Sheriff's deputies climbed into their cars as the small crowd dispersed.

Reed skidded to a stop next to Deputy Phillips's car, his breathing ragged. "Steve, wait." He doubled over and sucked in a deep breath. "What happened?"

The deputy shook his head and tucked a pen into his shirt pocket. "Jeffrey Kuhn shot himself."

"What?"

"Yeah. Right after a talk with your boss lady."

"Mona?"

"Yeah."

"Where is she? Is she okay?"

"She's fine. Left about fifteen minutes ago saying she'd be at the diner. She should be over there with the sheriff. He had a few questions for her."

"Did he cover the shooting?"

"No, he had a stop on the way back from delivering his mother to the hospital."

"Mother?"

"The Teague woman. Funny thing. I never knew it was his mother until I heard him and Toby talking about her. I didn't think much of it until I saw them together today at the diner. They look so much alike. Dangedest thing, those two never acted like mother and son." Steve glanced up at Reed. "I gotta go file my report. Did you need anything else?"

"Yeah, a ride over to the diner."

"Hop in." He cleared a space on the front seat.

Reed climbed in, wishing he was the one doing the driving. When they came in view of the diner, Mona's truck was gone.

"This is your stop." Steve shifted into park and waited for Reed to get out.

"Hold on a minute." He dialed Mona's cell phone, but she didn't answer. When he closed his phone, he noticed the message icon blinking. She must have left it while he was running and he hadn't heard it. He quickly called his voice mail and listened.

"Reed...on...way headed...Palo Duro Can—"

What sounded like a siren whined in the background and the message ended.

"Steve, can your report wait? I think Mona might be in trouble."

"I'm with you. Anything to put off writing those reports." Steve shifted in Reverse and pulled out of the diner parking lot. "Where to?"

WHEN THEY REACHED the hunter's cabin tucked between rock outcroppings in a lonely section of the canyon, Sheriff Parker Lee climbed out, opened the back door and pointed his service weapon at Mona. "Get out."

She sat still, afraid that if she got out, it would be all over. He'd kill her, and her baby would die as well. "I don't get it. Why?"

"It's not for you to understand. Just get out." He waved the gun impatiently.

"You were the ringleader of the cattle rustling all this time?" She'd figured Parker Lee was a horse's butt, a selfish, egotistical man with no thought to anyone but himself. But she'd never pegged him for a criminal. He was a sheriff. "You killed Dusty and Gil, didn't you?"

"Dusty saw too much and Gil knew too much."

"What about the salesman, Chase Molderhauer? Did you kill him too? Just so you could use his identity at the stockyards?" Sensing her unease, the baby kicked the inside of her belly. The sheriff was pure evil. She had to get away. Sitting in the back seat of his vehicle wasn't the way to do it. She prayed Reed got her message and was at that very minute speeding toward her.

"He tried to sell me an inferior knife he swore was an antique." Parker Lee's lip curled on one side. "It wasn't antique, but it was just as deadly."

Mona shivered at the image of the salesman with his throat slit from ear to ear. How she had ever fallen for Parker Lee, she couldn't fathom, and the more he revealed the more she wanted to throw up. "What about Deputy Jones?"

"Found out about my cattle truck. He had to go."

Sick, thinking about Tyler Jones's baby and wife having to live without him, Mona couldn't stand being in the same vehicle as the murdering sheriff. Escape became a necessity. She climbed out of the backseat, studying her surroundings.

The cabin probably dated back to the forties, the weathered wood hadn't been painted since…well, it probably had never felt the stroke of a paintbrush. The boards had shrunk so much from the rain, heat and cold that slices of shadowy black gaped between each. Prairie wind whipped at Mona's hair, slapping it against her face, as if warning her not to go nearer to the ancient structure. The clouds that had been building in the western sky encroached on the canyon, turning daylight to dusk.

Wisps of clouds dangled from the churning gray-green skies. Tornado weather. As if she didn't have enough troubles with a gun pointed at her.

The corner of a huge galvanized metal cattle trailer peeked out from behind a stand of rocks. Wayne and Les stepped out. Les carried a rifle and Wayne a .38 revolver with a pearl handle. Just like the one her father had given her. The one she'd dropped when she'd been surrounded by the four-wheelers just a short time ago.

"Nice gun, don't you think?" Wayne asked, twisting the weapon right then left, admiring the polished metal and pearl.

Mona pushed her anger aside. The gun wasn't as important as her baby's life. With three against one, her odds couldn't get much worse. Maybe she could talk to them until help arrived. Would help arrive? Hell, she didn't really know where she was, how could anyone else find her in the vastness of the canyon?

"Les, keep your rifle trained on her. Wayne, let me see that gun." Parker Lee held out his hand and waited for Wayne to lay the weapon in it. "Wayne, you know how important it is to follow orders, don't you?"

Wayne shifted and stared across at Les. "Yes, sir."

"When you don't, bad things happen, like to Dusty."

"That's right."

"Dusty was going to rat on us all, wasn't he?"

"Yeah."

"That's the trouble with too many people in the mix. Less is better."

"It is?" Wayne's eyes narrowed.

"Yeah." Parker aimed the weapon at Les. The man didn't even have time to react, before a loud crack ripped the air. Simultaneously, a flash of lightning was followed immediately by the rumble of thunder. The acrid scent of gunpowder stung Mona's nose.

Les Newton staggered backward and fell flat on his back, a circle of bright red blood forming on his forehead.

"What the hell did you do that for?" Wayne hesitated before lunging at Parker Lee. His hesitation cost him. Parker's next bullet clipped him in the temple.

Wayne Fennel dropped to the ground.

Mona didn't wait for the next shot. She threw herself behind the SUV, ducking low to avoid gunfire.

"Running won't do you much good, you know."

"Neither will standing there waiting for you to shoot me," she muttered.

"What was that? I couldn't hear you. Come on out. It's only a matter of time before your boyfriend gets here. I want to see the look on his face as you die."

"You're sick, Parker Lee. You aren't going to kill me." She dropped to the ground and peered under the chassis to locate his cowboy boots. He moved to the front of the car. Mona scooted around to the back. "You're not going to kill me because I'll kill you first." Her baby depended on her to stay alive. So what if it's father was a lunatic. The baby deserved a chance to live a normal, healthy life. "Why are you doing this? Is your mother putting you up to it?"

"My mother doesn't know anything. Because of what Grace Bryson and my father did the night before my parents' wedding, my mother suffered for a lifetime. She didn't deserve that kind of disrespect. I'm only making it right again."

"Grace and your father didn't kill anyone, Reed. Killing people isn't going to make anything right. It'll only put you in jail and cause your mother even more pain."

"No. You don't get it, do you? No one will know it was me. Your boyfriend will look like he was the one behind the cattle rustling and the murders." He rounded the passenger side of the SUV. Mona moved to the driver's side. The cabin was only ten feet away. If she could get inside, she could barricade the door and pray Reed got there soon. On the count of three. One…two…

Loose gravel shifted behind her. Mona flung herself toward the cabin, running as fast as her pregnant body could go. A gun exploded behind her, the bullet hitting the ground a yard to her right. She didn't stop. When she reached the door, she twisted the handle and pushed. It didn't budge. The ancient door had a brand-new lock on it and, presumably, Parker Lee was the owner of the key.

She spun to her left, looking for another avenue of escape, but before she could take another step, Parker Lee slammed into her, grasping her around the waist. *Not the baby. Don't hurt the baby.* Mona stopped fighting and went completely still. Praying he didn't notice, but knowing he couldn't help but guess.

"What the hell?" His arm jerked away from her belly, giving her just enough room to dodge around him.

He caught her by the hair and yanked her to a halt. "You're not going anywhere." His words were low and deadly.

Mona's scalp burned. He yanked again, sending her flying backward against him.

Lee spun her around and ripped her shirt open, his face a mottled red. "You're pregnant."

Mona grabbed the ends of her shirt and closed it over her nakedness. "No kidding."

"How far along?" he demanded.

"None of your business."

He pointed the gun at her belly. "Answer!"

Too afraid his fingers would slip on the trigger, Mona blurted, "Six months." The secret she'd tried so hard to keep was out. Her shoulders sagged. What did it matter? Parker Lee had no intention of letting her live. Not now. She knew too much. But she'd be damned if she went down without a fight. Graingers didn't quit.

Her gaze panned the area around the cabin, looking for something, anything she could use as a weapon. Two yards from where she stood, a gray, weathered board lay on the ground, a rusty nail sticking up out of it. With Parker Lee standing in front of her, holding a gun to her baby, could Mona get to it and beat some sense back into the sheriff's deranged skull?

REED'S FINGER dug into the armrest of the deputy's cruiser. "Can you go a little faster?"

"Any faster and I'll lose control." Despite his denial, Deputy Phillips pressed his foot to the floor, the car leaping forward, eating the miles between them and who knew what.

Mona had to be alive. Reed would accept no other option. She had too much determination and love in her to die so young. And she'd make a damn good mother to her baby. The child deserved a life with Mona as his mother.

The cruiser topped the rise and before them stretched the Palo Duro Canyon. Following the winding dirt road, they plunged downward into the maze of bluffs until a cabin came into sight.

His heart leaped into his throat when Reed realized the two people standing in front of the cabin were Sheriff Parker Lee and Mona. And the sheriff had a gun trained on Mona.

The deputy slammed on his brakes and skidded to a sideways stop, dust clouding the air.

Before the vehicle came to a complete stop, Reed flung the door open and jumped out.

"Oh good, just in time for the finale." Sheriff Lee grabbed Mona's arm and jerked it up behind her, pressing the gun to her forehead. "The bastard child of my father comes full circle to watch his life fall apart, just like my mother's."

"What is it you want, Lee?"

His eyes narrowed like a cat ready to pounce. "To watch you suffer."

How could Reed argue with that? The only way to end the suffering was to put a bullet in Sheriff Lee. But Lee had the upper hand. He had Mona.

"Drop your gun, Bryson."

Her shirt hung open, exposing the bulge of her baby and her breasts encased in a pale pink bra. Unfazed by her nakedness, Mona looked over at Reed. "Shoot him, Reed. He's going to kill you."

"I can't, baby." His heart broke at the fear in her eyes. The fear for his life.

"He's going to kill me anyway. Shoot him!" she shouted.

"You know I can't always be taking orders from a woman."

"Do it now, Reed." Tears tumbled down her cheeks. "Do it or you'll die."

"Put the gun down, Sheriff." Deputy Phillips raised his 9mm pistol and aimed it at the sheriff.

Sheriff Lee twisted, placing Mona between him and the deputy. "Shoot and you get the girl." He shrugged. "Which would play right into my hands. Now, put the weapon down, or she dies sooner."

Phillips maintained his hold on his gun. "No."

"Have it your way." Lee tugged on Mona's hair so hard tears filled her eyes and her head tipped back. He jammed the gun beneath her jaw.

"No!" Reed lunged forward.

"Drop the gun," the sheriff warned.

Mona shook her head, her eyes wild. "Don't do it, Reed."

Her captor smacked her face with the pistol barrel. "Shut up."

"I'm dropping the gun." Reed held his weapon trained on Parker. "Let her go. She didn't do anything to you."

"She's pregnant with my child and she didn't tell me. You call that nothing?"

"You don't care about the child." Reed inched forward.

"I'll be damned if another man raises him. I won't let it happen." Lee's face contorted, his teeth bared and his eyes shone glassy with unshed tears. "She should have told me." Lee shook her head so hard her teeth rattled.

"That hurts!" Mona jammed her elbow into Parker Lee's gut.

He grunted and loosened his hold enough that Mona broke free at the same time his gun went off.

Reed fired, the bullet hitting Parker Lee square in the chest, knocking him backward so hard he hit the cabin.

The sheriff pointed his gun at Reed and pulled the trigger.

Searing pain ripped through Reed's arm, jerking him away from the sheriff.

Mona bent to the ground and grabbed the weathered

two-by-four. When Sheriff Lee tried to aim at Reed again, Mona slammed the two-by-four across his arm.

Lee's forearm snapped, the gun flying from his grip. The man screamed and fell over, clutching at his arm, blood oozing from the wound to his chest, his face blanching a pale gray. "Bitch. I should have killed you."

She tossed the board to the side and kicked his gun far out of his reach. "Don't mess with the people I love."

"I should have killed you." Parker Lee's voice faded along with the color in his face.

"Get on the radio for Emergency Medical Services," Mona called out to Deputy Phillips. She hurried to Reed, tugging her shirt off her back to press into his wound. "Sit down, or you'll bleed out before the EMS gets here."

Reed smiled, dropping to the ground, his head getting dizzy. "Bossy woman."

"Not like it does me any good. You don't follow orders."

"I couldn't let him kill you," he said.

She cupped his cheek. "And I couldn't let him kill *you*."

"Guess your cattle rustling has come to an end."

Her eyes widened, a frown bringing her brows together. "Guess so."

"Still need a cowboy?"

A smile spread across her face, making her eyes

sparkle. "More than ever." Her gaze captured his, and she held her breath.

"Gonna advertise this time?"

Mona pinched his good arm. "No, the position is already filled." She leaned forward and brushed his lips with hers. "I hope."

"Damn right." Helicopter blades couldn't drown out the blood drumming in Reed's ears. Being with Mona was like coming home for good.

Epilogue

"Tommy, run down to the barn and tell your father that Papa and Nana are here." Mona stood on the porch, holding squirmy, six-month-old Sophia in her arms.

Grace and William Bryson parked in the driveway and climbed out of the car, one carrying a pie and the other a casserole dish.

"Good grief, Mom." Mona shook her head. "When I invite you two to dinner, I don't expect you to bring the food."

"You know she can't go anywhere empty handed." William smiled at his wife and helped her up the steps. Only a slight limp and a droopy eye remained as a reminder of Grace's stroke five years ago.

"Here, you take the pie. I want my granddaughter." Grace handed Mona the pie and relieved her of Sophia. "Where's Rosa, Fernando and Catalina?"

"Rosa and Catalina are inside setting the table, where I should be." Mona leaned into her daughter's face and kissed her nose. "Miss Sophia had other plans, didn't you? Fernando is with Reed down at the barn."

William glanced around the yard. "Where's my little man?"

At that moment, Reed, Fernando and Tommy rounded the corner of the house.

"Here I am!" Tomas William Bryson dropped his father's hand and raced into his papa's arms.

William lifted the child high into the air before settling him on his shoulders. "What have you been up to today?"

"I rode Dingo all by myself, didn't I, Daddy?"

Pride shone in Reed's eyes and smile. "Yes, you did, son. He rode all the way out to the north pasture and back."

"You're a regular cowboy, aren't you?" William said.

"Yes, sir." He looked at his mother. "I'm hungry, when do we get to eat?"

Mona laughed. "Not yet, sweetie. Not until the whole family is here."

A truck rumbled down the gravel driveway and pulled in next to William and Grace's car. Uncle Arty climbed down and smiled. "Is it too late? Did I miss the dinner bell?"

"No, Uncle Arty, you're just in time. Now that the whole family is here, we get to eat." Tommy wiggled free of his papa's arms and ran for the house.

Mona stared around at the people she considered her family gathered on the porch and at the cowboy who'd made her family so full and complete. Her heart swelled with love and happiness.

Everyone filed into the house for dinner. Reed held the door for her, but she didn't go in immediately.

"What are you thinking?"

"What a wonderful husband you are, and what a terrific father you are to Tommy and Sophia."

"I love them, just like I love their mother." He pulled Mona into his arms and dropped a kiss on her forehead.

She laughed, shaking her head.

Reed's eyes narrowed. "What?"

"It's funny to think it all started with one newspaper ad."

"Lady, I think your ad-writing days are over." He pulled her into his arms and kissed her, wiping all thoughts of ads completely out of her mind.

* * * * *

Enjoy a sneak preview of
MATCHMAKING WITH A MISSION
by B.J. Daniels, part of the
WHITEHORSE, MONTANA *miniseries.*
Available from Harlequin Intrigue
in April 2008.

Nate Dempsey has returned to Whitehorse to uncover the truth about his past…

Nate sensed someone watching the house and looked out in surprise to see a woman astride a paint horse just on the other side of the fence. He quickly stepped back from the filthy second-floor window, although he doubted she could have seen him. Only a little of the June sun pierced the dirty glass to glow on the dust-coated floor at his feet as he waited a few heartbeats before he looked out again.

The place was so isolated he hadn't expected to see another soul. Like the front yard, the dirt road was waist-high with weeds. When he'd broken the lock on the back door, he'd had to kick aside a pile of rotten leaves that had blown in from last fall.

As he sneaked a look, he saw that she was still there, staring at the house in a way that unnerved him. He shielded his eyes from the glare of the sun off the dirty window and studied her, taking in her head of long blond hair that feathered out in the breeze from under her Western straw hat.

She wore a tan canvas jacket, jeans and boots. But it was the way she sat astride the brown-and-white horse that nudged the memory.

He felt a chill as he realized he'd seen her before. In that very spot. She'd been just a kid then. A kid on a pretty paint horse. Not this one—the markings were different. Anyway, it couldn't have been the same horse, considering the last time he had seen her was more than twenty years ago. That horse would be dead by now.

His mind argued it probably wasn't even the same girl. But he knew better. It was the way she sat the horse, so at home in a saddle and secure in her world on the other side of that fence.

To the boy he'd been, she and her horse had represented freedom, a freedom he'd known he would never have—even after he escaped this house.

Nate saw her shift in the saddle, and for a moment he feared she planned to dismount and come toward the house. With Ellis Harper in his grave, there would be little to keep her away.

To his relief, she reined her horse around and rode back the way she'd come.

As he watched her ride away, he thought about the way she'd stared at the house—today and years ago. While the smartest thing she could do was to stay clear of this house, he had a feeling she'd be back.

Finding out her name should prove easy, since he figured she must live close by. As for her interest in Harper House… He would just have to make sure it didn't become a problem.

* * * * *

Be sure to look for
MATCHMAKING WITH A MISSION
and other suspenseful
Harlequin Intrigue stories,
available in April wherever books are sold.

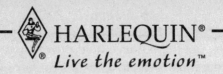

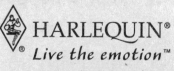

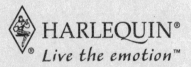

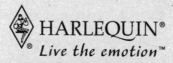

HARLEQUIN®
Presents®

**The world's bestselling romance series...
The series that brings you your favorite authors,
month after month:**

Helen Bianchin...Emma Darcy
Lynne Graham...Penny Jordan
Miranda Lee...Sandra Marton
Anne Mather...Carole Mortimer
Susan Napier...Michelle Reid

and many more uniquely talented authors!

Wealthy, powerful, gorgeous men...
Women who have feelings just like your own...
The stories you love, set in exotic, glamorous locations...

HARLEQUIN®
Presents®

Seduction and Passion Guaranteed!

HPDIR104

Harlequin® Historical
Historical Romantic Adventure!

*Imagine a time of chivalrous
knights and unconventional ladies,
roguish rakes and impetuous
heiresses, rugged cowboys
and spirited frontierswomen—
these rich and vivid tales will
capture your imagination!*

*Harlequin Historical . . .
they're too good to miss!*

SPECIAL EDITION™

Emotional, compelling stories that capture the intensity of living, loving and creating a family in today's world.

Modern, passionate reads that are powerful and provocative.

nocturne

Dramatic and sensual tales of paranormal romance.

Romances that are sparked by danger and fueled by passion.

SDIR07